"Got a second?" Luca

"About that," Kai ans

"I doubt Lucas would have made it to the finals today if you hadn't pushed him these last few weeks," Buzzy said.

Kai nodded silently and glanced at the crowd on the beach. Almost everyone was facing out toward the water, watching the surfers.

"But maybe you've pushed him far enough," Buzzy said.

Kai turned and looked at him. "What do you mean?"

"Everyone knows you don't care that much about competing," Buzzy said. "In a way, if you win today, it's almost a waste, because you probably won't do anything with it."

"You want me to let Lucas win because you think he'll do more with it than I will?" Kai cut to the chase.

"Why not?" Buzzy said. "You've done it before."

**Check out all the books in the
Impact Zone series:**

**Take Off
Cut Back
Close Out**

Available from Simon Pulse

**And get hooked on some of Todd Strasser's
other Simon & Schuster books . . .**

*Can't Get There from Here
Give a Boy a Gun
How I Created My Perfect Prom Date
Here Comes Heavenly
Buzzard's Feast: Against the Odds*

IMPACT ZONE
CLOSE OUT

TODD STRASSER

Simon Pulse

New York   London   Toronto   Sydney

First Simon Pulse edition July 2004

Text copyright © 2004 by Todd Strasser

SIMON PULSE
An imprint of Simon & Schuster
Children's Publishing Division
1230 Avenue of the Americas
New York, NY 10020

Designed by Ann Sullivan
The text of this book was set in Bembo.

Printed in the United States of America
10 9 8 7 6 5 4 3 2 1

Library of Congress Control Number 2004100034

ISBN 0-689-87031-0

One

Flat again.

Kai and Bean were sitting around a picnic table on the terrace outside Pete's Hubba Hubba Seaside Saloon, eating chili cheese fries. In the slanting late-afternoon sunlight, Bean tapped his fingers against the tabletop with uncharacteristic nervousness. He gave Kai a questioning look. "You're *sure* you want to do it tonight?"

Kai gazed out at the horizon, where the dark blue water met the light blue sky. Here and there a cotton ball pink-edged white cloud dotted the blue heavens. The ocean was as still and flat as a photograph. He looked back at his friend. "I have to, Bean. I don't think I have a choice."

Before Bean could reply, Booger joined them at the table. "Can you believe this?" he complained, pointing at the ocean. "It's been like glass for five days."

"Toilet bowl water," said Bean.

It was dinnertime and the terrace at Pete's was crowded with teens in shorts and bathing suits, talking loudly, laughing, chatting on cell phones. Lately Kai had been taking as long as he wanted for dinner. Strangely, his father, Big Chief Hockaloogie, didn't seem to care. But this evening was going to be a major test of the Alien Frog Beast's patience.

The air was tranquil and warm, the beach still crowded despite the late hour, as if the Sun Haven vacationers couldn't tear themselves away from such a beautiful scene. The brightly colored umbrellas that had stood open like flowers all day in the bright sun were now closed, poking up from the sand like skinny trees. The ocean was smooth except for the random spots where bluefish had forced bait fish to the surface and were causing the water to boil in the massacre.

Bean let out a loud sigh. Just moments ago, before Booger joined them, Kai had quietly told him the plan for that evening. The tall, thin eighteen-year-old with the long braided black ponytail was not happy.

"What's with all the sighing and finger tapping?" Booger asked him.

"Uh, nothing." Bean straightened up self-consciously. "Just itching to surf again. That's all."

The door from the saloon to the terrace swung open and Everett, the dreadlocked black kid from Lucas Frank's crew, stepped out with a drink in one hand and a red-and-white-striped paper box of chili cheese fries in the other. The door swung closed behind him and Everett stood for a moment, scanning the patio for a place to sit.

Kai waved at him. For an instant Everett didn't react. As if he had to make a major decision. And the truth was that, in a way, maybe he did.

Everett started toward them. Kai slid over on the bench to make room at the picnic table.

"You guys know Everett, right?" Kai said.

Booger and Bean nodded. Kai was pretty sure that both of them realized that Everett joining them was a major deal.

The dreadlocked kid sat down and nodded

toward the beach and the vast blue liquid flatness stretching to the horizon. "What a drag, huh?"

Only another surfer would understand what he meant. Otherwise, it looked like a beautiful summer evening beach scene.

"The calm before the storm," said Bean.

Booger looked up, excited, and asked, "There's a storm coming?" Again only a surfer would understand that a storm was something to be welcomed. The funny thing was, Kai knew Bean was referring to something that had nothing to do with the weather. Instead, it had to do with a certain "mission" they were going to undertake later that evening.

"In a couple of weeks hurricane season'll start," Everett said. "Best time of year."

The patio door swung open again and Shauna came out with a drink and a chili cheese dog. Wearing a bright green T-shirt that read I SCREAM FOR ICE CREAM, she was on her dinner break from her job making cones and sundaes.

"Hey, guys." She sat down and smiled at everyone as if it was perfectly normal to find Everett there.

"Shauna, you know Everett, right?" Kai said.

"I don't think we've ever been, uh, formally introduced," Shauna said. "So, hi, I'm Shauna, otherwise known as the newbie kook surf chick."

"I've seen you out there catching waves," Everett said. "You're gettin' it."

Shauna lit up with pride. "That's it, guys. My day's just been made." She looked around. "Where's Spazzy?"

"Jillian said they were going to a movie," Bean said. "They like to go at dinnertime during the week, when there won't be as many people around to freak out when Spazzy does his thing."

"So I hear you really ripped at the Fairport contest," Everett said to Kai.

"Best single-wave score of the day," Bean said, patting Kai proudly on the shoulder.

Everett turned to Bean. "And you took first in the long board."

"Considering that there were only five long boarders in the whole contest, I'm not sure that means a whole lot," Bean said.

"That roundhouse cutback you finished with would have scored huge points anywhere," Kai said.

"What's this about you getting yourself

disqualified on purpose?" Everett said to Kai. "So Spazzy could get into the final."

"Meant a lot more to him than it would have to me," Kai answered with a shrug. "So how come you weren't at Fairport?"

Everett grinned. "Remember how fine the waves were that day? Think about what Screamers was like without all you mutts stinking up the place."

"You had Screamers to yourself the *whole day*?" Booger let his jaw drop in exaggerated surprise.

"Just about," Everett said. "Sure beat sitting on the beach at Fairport waiting for a twenty-minute heat once every two hours."

"That settles it, dudes," Booger said. "I know where I'm gonna be next time there's a surf competition around here."

"Where's that?" someone behind them asked.

They turned to find Jade, the shapely young woman who worked the counter at Sun Haven Surf. She was wearing pink shorts and a skimpy green bikini top that was clearly stretched to the limit by the twin demands placed upon it. Booger, especially, appeared transfixed by the sight.

"Uh, here at Beamers," he stammered. "I mean, Screamers."

"Well, guess what?" Jade handed them sheets of bright orange paper. "You won't be alone. It's gonna get pretty crowded around here."

Kai read the handout. The $5,000 Northeast Open Surfing Championship was going to be held at Sun Haven at the end of August, sponsored by Sun Haven Surf, Quiksilver, Roxy, O'Neill, Sex Wax, Pro Traction, Bonzo Kreem, and other companies. Top prize in each category was $500, except the men's short board, which would be $1,000 with a second prize of $500.

Across the table Booger had not yet looked at the handout. He was still staring at Jade. Bean folded his sheet into a paper airplane and hit Booger in the forehead.

"Hey!" Booger yelped in surprise.

"It's not polite to stare," Bean lectured him.

Booger's face turned bright red. He looked down at his french fries. "Sorry."

"Oh, I don't mind guys staring," Jade said, shooting a quick glance at Kai. "Especially the right guy."

Shauna crossed her arms and pouted.

"Could I be the right guy?" Booger looked up and asked eagerly.

"Sorry."

"Aw." Booger's shoulders slumped.

Jade pressed her finger down on one of the orange handouts lying on the table. "This is the one competition you don't want to get yourself disqualified from," she said to Kai. "It's the biggest deal of the year around here. Prize money, media coverage. Guys even pick up sponsorships."

"I bet that's not *all* they pick up," Shauna muttered.

The patio door swung open again. Lucas Frank came out, followed by Slammin' Sam and that quiet guy, Derek. All three of them were carrying drinks and white paper plates with chili cheeseburgers and chili cheesesteak sandwiches. Lucas seemed to hesitate when he saw Kai and his friends, as if he wasn't sure whether to go over or just ignore them. He focused on Everett, and Kai assumed he was wondering why a kid from his crew would be sitting with Kai and his friends.

It was Sam who started toward them.

"Hey, there he is," he said to Kai. "Mr.

Competition. What happened at Fairport, tuna, the pressure get to you? Was it just too much for the chicken of the sea?"

Kai stared at the big jerk. Slowly and deliberately he started to get up. "I told you what would happen if you ever called me that again."

TWO

Bench legs screeched against the concrete patio as half a dozen people jumped up and placed themselves between Sam and Kai. The entire terrace outside Pete's went silent as everyone became aware of the sudden potential for violence. Kai had no intention of struggling against the hands he felt pressing on his shoulders and gripping his arms. He just wanted to get eye to eye with Sam.

"I'm not going to fight," he calmly told Bean and Everett, who were among those holding him back. He felt the hands on his arms loosen and the bodies slowly move out of the way until he and Sam faced each other. Sam had a strange look in his eye. Half aggro, half puzzlement.

"I think you and I should have a talk," Kai said.

"I said everything I got to say to you," Sam taunted.

"Then maybe you should shut up and listen," Kai said. He felt the hands on his arms tighten again. Sam bristled.

"If you want to fight, just tell me when and where and I'll be there," Kai said. "It's that simple, okay? But in the meantime, you have to stop calling me these dumb-ass names. This isn't kindergarten, dude. You have to grow up."

It was so quiet you could hear the scratching of the small brown sparrows who snuck under the tables and pecked at crumbs. Sam's face was red. Kai could see the guy's pulse throb under the black barbwire tattoo around his neck.

"Well?" Kai said.

"Fuck you." Sam turned away and headed toward another table.

The tension on the terrace slowly evaporated like an early-morning fog under the rays of a rising sun. People at other tables began to talk again. Kai's friends sat down. The sparrows hopped away and flew out of reach. Sam had gone, but Lucas remained standing near the table. He kept looking at Everett as if he couldn't understand why one of his brahs was sitting with Kai and his friends.

Lucas held up the orange handout announcing the Northeast Championship. "What about this?"

"I don't know," Kai said. "Just found out about it."

"Yeah, yeah," said Sam, who'd stopped between two tables a short distance away. "We've heard that one before. You gotta think about it. You always gotta think about everything. I never saw anyone who spent so much time thinking."

"Maybe I'm setting an example for you, Sam," Kai said. "You might want to try it one of these days."

The people around them chuckled. Sam clenched his teeth in angry frustration and stomped away.

"This is as big as it gets around here," Lucas said, gesturing to the handout. "You do well in the regional championship and you might qualify for the nationals. Then invitations start coming in. Florida, California, Hawaii. Just think, dude. This could be your ticket back home."

"Could be," Kai allowed.

"Bet *that's* something worth thinking about," Lucas said. He turned to Everett and motioned to another picnic table where Sam and Derek were now sitting, eating their sandwiches and fries. "Come on, dude, we're sitting over there."

Everett didn't budge. The lines between Lucas's eyes narrowed. Everett was one of his crew, and this was a serious breach. Kai caught Everett's eye and motioned that he'd understand if Everett decided to join his brahs. But Everett merely picked up a french fry and bit it in half. He looked up at Lucas. The gaze Lucas returned was hard, as if he was trying to stare the guy down. Everett didn't blink.

"Thanks, but I think I'll hang here today," he said.

Lucas's forehead bunched ever so slightly. Then he turned toward the table where Derek and Sam were sitting. For a moment, no one at Kai's table said a word.

Kai flattened the orange handout on the table. "What do you guys think?"

"There's no bodyboard competition," Booger said. "Otherwise I'd do it. What would I have to lose?"

"What about the long board competition?" Shauna asked Bean.

"Sure, why not?" Bean said.

Kai turned to Everett. "What about you?"

Everett shook his head. "There's no point for me. I've never been into hard turns and slash-and-bash. Everyone knows that's how the judges score. I wouldn't make it past the first heat. But you .... Based on how you did at Fairport, you could be a real contender."

"I just don't know if that's what I want to be," Kai said.

"There's time to decide," Bean said.

At the mention of time, Shauna checked her watch. "Break's almost over. I have to get back to work."

"Me too." Everett started to get up.

"Where do you work?" Kai asked.

"Blockbuster," Everett said.

"Hey, that's where I'm headed," Booger said. "I'll go with you."

Suddenly the only ones left at the table were Bean and Kai.

"Guess it's time for us to go," Kai said.

Bean leaned close and spoke in a low voice. "It's breaking the law, you know."

"How's that?" Kai asked.

"I'm not exactly sure," Bean said. "I just have a feeling. There's still time for you to change your mind about this."

Kai slowly shook his head. "I already told you, Bean, this is something I have to do. But there's time for you to change *your* mind."

"Do you want me to change my mind?" Bean asked.

"No."

Bean sighed and heaved himself up from the bench. "Then come on, let's get it over with."

Three

The meeting place was the parking lot of a large, red barnlike club called 88s located on Seaside Drive about halfway between Sun Haven and Belle Harbor. The big white sign with black letters announced LIVE MUSIC NIGHTLY.

Bean pulled the hearse into the parking lot and shut off the engine. The sun was low in the western sky, but had not yet begun to turn the orange of sunset. There was probably an hour of light left. Except for a few cars, the club's parking lot was empty.

"He's not here," Bean said, craning his neck and looking around.

"He'll come," said Kai.

Bean slumped in his seat and leaned his head against the headrest. "You know, it's weird, Kai. I've lived in this town all my life and it's pretty much always been the same. The cool locals have always owned Screamers. The rest of us have been stuck with Sewers. Guys like Buzzy Frank have ruled this town, and Curtis has always been a thorn in their sides. Every summer Spazzy would come down and watch us, but no one ever talked to him. That's just the way things have always been. Nothing ever changed. Then you show up and everything changes."

"For the better, I hope," Kai said.

"I hope so too," Bean said as a familiar-looking red Jeep pulled into the parking lot. "But at this particular moment I have serious doubts."

The Jeep pulled next to the hearse. Goldilocks, the guy with the long bleached-blond dreadlocks, waved at them to join him.

"Here we go." Kai reached for the door handle.

"Whoopee-do," Bean grumbled.

They got out of the hearse and walked over to the Jeep.

"Get in," Goldilocks said.

Bean reached for the back to climb in, but Kai got there first and gave him a look as if he wanted Bean to sit in the front. Bean frowned, but did it. Goldilocks pulled the Jeep out of the parking lot and got on Seaside Drive heading toward Belle Harbor. Kai felt the wind on his face as the Jeep cruised down the road.

"So you guys like to surf, huh?" Goldilocks asked over the wind noise.

"Yeah," Kai answered. "How about you?"

"I do a little surfing, but I'm more of a collector and trader," Goldilocks answered. He slowed the Jeep down and then made a left off Seaside Drive onto a narrower, paved road. The road formed a boundary between a forest of oak and pine to the right, and a wide field of grass on the left. Kai thought it must have been a sod farm. Goldilocks pulled the Jeep onto the shoulder of the road. Kai and Bean watched silently while he reached into a glove compartment and pulled out two blue bandannas.

"Around your eyes, dudes." Goldilocks handed the bandannas to Bean and Kai.

"We going to your secret spot?" Kai asked.

"Just put them on," Goldilocks said.

Kai and Bean pulled the bandannas over their eyes and tied them in the back. When the

Jeep lurched back onto the road, it caught Kai by surprise, and he quickly grabbed for a handhold and started to count silently.

After a while Kai felt the Jeep slow down and make a right turn. The ride became a lot bumpier and the Jeep lurched and rattled loudly. Kai was pretty sure they were on a dirt road. He started counting again, and stopped when they slowed and made a left. Then he started once again. This part of the ride was even bumpier, and with his eyes covered by the bandanna Kai began to feel woozy with each unexpected bounce and drop.

Finally the Jeep stopped.

"Okay, take 'em off," Goldilocks said.

Kai pulled the bandanna off. They were deep in the woods. The spaces between the trees were thick with brush. It seemed to Kai that they were in a place where few people generally ventured. It was quiet. As dusk approached, the air was still and the sunlight was beginning to drain away.

Without a word Goldilocks started into the woods. Kai and Bean followed. At first Kai couldn't tell where they were headed, but then he saw a small green wooden shed with a sagging roof, nestled in the trees.

Goldilocks stopped and pulled some keys out of his pocket. The old wooden doors were held together with a locked latch, which he released, allowing the doors to swing open.

Except for the thin bars of light that seeped in through cracks and gaps in the walls, it was dark inside the shed. There was barely enough light for Kai to see that the dozen or so surfboards lying on their rails inside were almost certainly the same ones he'd first seen in Curtis's shed a few months before. He recognized the light blue Bruce Jones, the plain off-white Rusty, and the custom boards that appeared to have no markings whatsoever.

Kai stepped closer and carefully leaned one of the plain custom boards back so that he could see the stringer. There were the letters *TL* and #174. The board next to it was #239. So all these years Curtis had been collecting Teddy's boards. Somehow Kai wasn't surprised.

"What do you think?" Goldilocks said.

"These things are beautiful," Kai said. "So you just collected them over the years?"

"Sort of, yeah," Goldilocks said.

"Where's the good breaks around here?" Kai asked innocently.

"What do you mean, breaks?" Goldilocks asked.

Kai shot Bean a quick look. What kind of surfer didn't know what a break was?

"I meant, where do you surf around here?" Kai asked.

"Oh, you know, up and down the beach."

Kai ran his fingers down the rail of the Bruce Jones board as if he was admiring it. "They got a surf shop in Belle Harbor?"

"Naw, most people go over to that place in Sun Haven," Goldilocks said.

"Sun Haven Surf?" Kai pretended to act surprised.

"Yeah, that's it."

Kai spoke to Bean. "You know who'd love to take a look at these boards? Buzzy."

Goldilocks didn't react.

"You know Buzzy?" Kai asked him.

Goldilocks shook his head. Either the guy was a really good actor, or Kai's hunch that Buzzy Frank was somehow involved in the theft of Curtis's boards was going down the toilet fast. It was Bean who came to his rescue.

"Know who else would love to get his hands on these?" he said. "Big Dave McAllister."

"The guy who runs the board room?" Kai

said, watching Goldilocks out of the corner of his eye.

"Yeah."

This time Kai caught the flicker in Goldilocks's eye. If you weren't looking for it, you might not have noticed. But there was no missing the abrupt change in the guy's attitude.

"So look, what's the story here?" he asked, suddenly impatient. "Are we gonna make a deal? You gonna buy a board or what?"

"Know what I'd really like to do?" Kai said. "I'd really like to get Big Dave over here to see these things. He'd know what they were worth."

"Hey, screw Big Dave, okay?" Goldilocks snarled. "You guys surf. You don't need him to know what a good board looks like. And he'd say the same thing."

Kai pretended to be confused. "You know Big Dave?"

"Uh . . . No, never heard of him," Goldilocks said. "So what's the deal? You want a board or not?"

"Do I want one?" Kai repeated. "Sure. But I don't know what they're worth, so how do I know what to pay?"

"How much money do you have?" Goldilocks asked.

"Man, these are nice boards," Kai said. "I'm sure I don't have enough."

"How much?" Goldilocks pressed.

Kai felt himself being backed into a corner. "I don't know."

"You don't know how much money you have?"

"Well, I . . . I didn't really bring any," Kai said.

Goldilocks turned to Bean. "You're the one with the money?"

"Forty or fifty bucks," Bean answered.

"What the fuck?" Goldilocks sputtered. "You guys came here to look at these boards, but you didn't bring enough money to buy one? So why'd you come?"

Kai shot Bean a look, as if he desperately needed help with an answer.

"Hey, don't look at him," Goldilocks said. "What's going on here? What do you guys want?"

"Boards," Bean said in a quavering voice.

"For forty or fifty bucks?" Goldilocks said. "You knew that wasn't enough."

"I . . . I was scared," Bean said.

Goldilocks frowned. "Of what?"

"That you were gonna rip us off," Bean said.

"Like how did we know this wasn't a scam?" Kai asked, following Bean's lead. "Maybe you were gonna take us all the way out here into the woods and rob us."

Strangely, this admission helped calm Goldilocks down. "I gotcha. So I'd bring you out here, take your money and leave you." He seemed to like the idea that Kai and Bean thought he was a badass dude. "So now what? We go back to your car, right? Because that's where you left the money?"

Kai and Bean glanced at each other. They both shook their heads.

"The money's not in the car?" Goldilocks asked, confused.

"What would have stopped you from taking us back to the car and robbing us there?" Kai asked.

Instead of answering, Goldilocks pulled the shed doors closed and relocked the latch. "Okay, let's go."

Once again they were blindfolded. This time the ride was faster and bumpier. Sitting in the back, Kai felt as if he would have been bounced clear out of the Jeep if he hadn't held on.

It wasn't long before they were back in the parking lot at 88s. By now the sun had turned reddish orange and had dropped close to the horizon. Kai and Bean climbed out of the Jeep. In the deepening light, Kai could see that Bean looked a bit green after the bumpy, blindfolded ride.

"Okay," Goldilocks said. "So you've seen the boards. Next time I hear from you guys, it's gonna be because you've got the money, right? Otherwise, don't waste my fricken time."

The Jeep's wheels screeched and spun, spitting back loose gravel. Goldilocks took off, leaving a cloud of dust and exhaust.

"You okay?" Kai asked Bean.

"Great," Bean grumbled, reaching for the hearse's door. "Just great."

Kai got in on the passenger side and Bean started to drive back toward Sun Haven. Kai's friend had a sour look on his face. "That's the end, dude," he said. "I mean it. I hate dealing with creeps like that. Don't ever ask me to do something like that again, understand?"

"I thought we made a good team," Kai

said as he opened the glove compartment and started hunting through the paperbacks.

"Team? What are you talking about? You're insane. Reality check. We are *not a team*, get it? No way am I ever dealing with a creep like Goldilocks again. Ever!"

"Got a piece of paper?" Kai asked.

"Any piece of paper?" Bean asked. "Or a certificate of insanity? Because you are certifiable, know that? And so am I for going along with you."

"Hey, two peas in a pod." Kai tore a blank sheet from the back of one of the paperback books. "Got a pen?"

"Writing a will?" Bean asked.

"Chill, Bean, we found out what we needed to know, and we got away unhurt," Kai said. "I'd say the mission was a success. Now, seriously, a pen?"

Bean reached up to the sun visor. On the other side was a plastic pocket with some pens and pencils. He handed one to Kai. "Mission? Dude, this isn't a video game. That Goldilocks is one serious badass and he's not—"

Kai pressed a finger to his lips. "Quiet. I have to remember."

"Remember what?"

"Where we were and how we got there." Kai started to write.

"What are you talking about?" Bean said. "We were blindfolded."

"I know." Kai started to write down each turn they'd made and how long he'd counted between them.

"What are you doing?" Bean asked suspiciously.

"Writing down the directions."

"Directions?"

"Yeah," Kai said. "For when we go back."

Four

Bean was silent for the rest of the ride to Sun Haven. By the time they got there, the sun was well below the horizon and it was getting dark.

"This is the last time I'm gonna say this," Bean said as they cruised into town. "You're a great guy and a good friend, but I've had it with the cops and robbers stuff. It's over, done, finished. Next time, find someone else to risk his life, because I've retired."

He pulled the hearse to the curb and stopped. "Here you go."

Kai looked out the window. They were in front of T-licious. For a second Kai didn't recognize the place.

"You didn't tell me your old man was getting into the surf clothes business," Bean said.

Kai stared at the storefront. He hadn't told Bean because he didn't know himself. The store not only had a new look, but a new name. It was no longer T-licious Custom T-shirts. It was now T-licious Discount Surf Wear and Custom T-shirts. Displayed in the window were long-sleeved T-shirts and rash guards from some of the top surf apparel companies like Roxy, Hurley, Quiksilver, and Billabong. In addition, stuck here and there to the glass were bright red stickers proclaiming SALE! OVERRUNS! OFF-PRICE! MANUFACTURER'S SECONDS! DEEP DISCOUNTS!

Looking through the window and into the shop, Kai saw plenty of customers picking through the racks and displays. Most were kids.

He reached for the hearse's door handle, then looked back at Bean. "I really appreciate your help."

"Oh, yeah?" Bean said. "Well, please show your appreciation by never asking me to do anything like that again."

Kai smiled. "Did anyone ever tell you that you're cute when you're angry?"

"Get out," Bean growled.

"Catch you later?" Kai asked.

"Sorry, I've got plans," Bean said. "Non-life-threatening ones, for a change."

Kai got out of the hearse, walked across the sidewalk and stepped into the shop. Dick Dale's "Miserlou," the anthem of 1960s California surf culture, was playing on a boom box. It was clear that Pat had jumped on the surf craze bandwagon that was currently selling millions of dollars of surf apparel to kids in landlocked states thousands of miles from the ocean who wouldn't have known a beer keg from a board skeg.

Even more amazing, there was actually a line to the cash register where Pat was merrily ringing up sales while Sean rushed to and from the back office where, Kai assumed, he was running off extra credit card slips for Pat's "business associates" in Nevada.

Kai caught his father's eye, but knew better than to interrupt him when he was doing business. The Alien Frog Beast gave his son a hard look, and Kai knew he was ticked off that he hadn't been around that evening to assist in the scam. Kai wandered over to a rack loaded with rash guards. He still hadn't been able to scrape together the money to buy one for himself, and instead had been surfing bare-chested or in a T-shirt. The one he liked at Sun Haven Surf, an aqua blue polyolefin/spandex long-sleeve made by O'Neill, was listed at close to seventy-five dollars—far more than he could afford.

Kai thumbed through the rack. All the familiar brands were there. He stopped at an aqua blue long-sleeved O'Neill rash guard almost exactly like the one at Sun Haven Surf, except his father was selling this one for thirty-four ninety-five. How could they sell the same garment for half what Buzzy sold it for? Kai pulled the rash guard off the rack. Up close he could see that the O'Neill logo wasn't quite the right size or in quite the same place as the one he'd seen in Sun Haven Surf. The seams were loosely sewn and the material felt thin and rough.

Kai slid the rash guard back into the rack. After two years of living with a crook like Pat, he could pretty easily figure out what the story was. These items weren't manufacturer's seconds, made of the same material but with a flaw that kept them from being sold in regular stores. These garments were knockoffs, imitations made as cheaply as possible out of inferior materials, and stamped with counterfeit logos.

Leave it to his father to concoct a scam like this.

Kai went into the back office where Sean was running extra credit card slips.

"Hey, Kai, where ya been?" his half brother asked. "Dad's ticked that you didn't come back after dinner."

Kai shrugged. "Looks like the new scam is a big success."

"It ain't a scam," Sean said. "He explained the whole thing to me. Manufacturer's seconds."

It always amazed Kai that his half brother was so gullible. "And where'd he get these so-called seconds?"

"You know," Sean said. "That place in Brooklyn."

"The place where the guys have those strange bulges under their shirts near their waists?" Kai said.

"I asked Dad about that," Sean said. "He told me Brooklyn's a really dangerous place. Those guys need guns to protect themselves."

Kai had serious doubts about that, but didn't see the point in arguing. Nor did he think it was worth pointing out that the guys with the strange bulges under their shirts insisted on dealing only in cash and avoided all forms of paperwork—not exactly the typical way of doing business.

Sean went out to the front of the store and closed the door behind him. Kai stayed in the back. He didn't want to be out front where he would be expected to help sell this bogus crap to unsuspecting tourists. Instead he sat down at the computer and clicked onto Ethan's Web site. Ethan, his mom's boyfriend until her death two years before, was a photographer back on Kauai.

Ethan's site uploaded slowly. Kai's father, the cheapest person on earth, still insisted on using a dial-up connection to the Internet. Finally the page appeared, featuring a beautiful fiery pink sunset shot of Bali Hai, the mountainous point where the road on the north shore of the island ended and the steep, rocky shoreline of the Na Pali coast began.

Kai sat back and gazed up at the ceiling. His mom used to take him hiking along the Na Pali coast, along rocky jungle trails that were overgrown with green vegetation and had a view of the vast endlessly blue Pacific with the sound of waves smashing into white foam against the rocks below. They'd often stopped for lunch on the cliffs, and if it was winter, they might see the humpback whales who'd come down from Alaska to give birth to calves. Kai knew that a lot of kids thought whale watching was pretty cheesy, but once you'd actually seen those huge beasts—the largest animals on earth—you might change your mind.

He looked at the computer again. Ethan's site had contact information. Kai only had to tap a few keys to send him an e-mail. He felt that tug. Ethan was a great guy. While Pat, Big Chief Hockaloogie, may have been his birth father, there was no doubt in Kai's mind that Ethan was his real father. *But then Kai's mom had died. . . .*

The door opened and Pat came in. Kai quickly closed the Web site, but not before his father got a look.

"Still dreaming about going back, huh?" his father said.

Kai was tightlipped.

"Well, dream on, sonny boy, because it ain't gonna happen," the Alien Frog Beast gloated. "What the hell would that Ethan guy want with you? You ain't his kid. That's over. Wake up and smell the bacon."

Kai fought the temptation to ball his hands into fists and hit him with all his might. Birth father or no birth father.

"Get up," Pat said.

"Why?" Kai asked.

"Why the hell do you think?" Pat snapped. "I need you out front to help sell. You see how crowded it is out there?"

"I guess people must really love those cheap knockoffs," Kai said.

Pat's eyes narrowed menacingly. "Well, ain't you one observant little punk."

"You're doing this just to give Buzzy Frank as much grief as you can, aren't you?" Kai asked. "I mean, it's not even about the money. Buzzy forced you to pay all the rent up front, and you're so pissed off, you'll do anything to get back at him. I'm surprised you didn't just firebomb his store."

"Why? So he can collect insurance?" Pat asked. "Overstate the damages and then make a mint on the fire sale? I'm not doing that guy any favors."

Kai resisted the urge to laugh. Only his father could look at torching someone's store as doing that person a favor.

"Did it ever occur to you that not every-body is totally dishonest?" Kai asked. "That not everybody goes around looking for every pos-sible opportunity to scam the rest of the world."

Pat grinned, revealing his cruddy little yel-low teeth. "Hell, yes, sonny boy, if everybody was a scammer, there'd be no one left to scam. Thank the lord there are more of them than there are of me." But the grin turned hard. "Now, you gonna help sell or not?"

The stale air in the back room grew still. Kai suddenly realized that he'd come to a turn-ing point. He didn't know how or why it was happening at this very moment, but it was.

"Not," he answered.

The Alien Frog Beast Chief Hockaloogie stared at him for a long time, as if he too understood what this meant. Then he held out his hand. "The keys."

Kai reached into his pocket and pulled out his key ring. He removed the store key and tossed it in the air. His father caught it. *Good riddance,* Kai thought. He never wanted to set foot in this store again.

But his father reached out again. "And the apartment key."

This time Kai hesitated. As if the meaning of his father's words wasn't completely obvious, Pat decided to spell it out for him. "This is the end, sonny boy. I've had all the crap from you I'm gonna take. You don't want to play on my team, fine. You go find another team. And that means another place to live."

"Before I give you the key," Kai said, "there are some things I'd like to get first."

Pat's hand closed into a fist. "Make it fast."

Five

For once Kai did as his father said. Almost as if he didn't want to take the time to think too much about it for fear that he'd change his mind. He walked to the house with the basement apartment he and his father and Sean had recently moved into. On the way, he passed the Driftwood Motel. The office was dark and the no vacancy sign was on. Kai went a few more blocks, let himself into the apartment, got his things, and headed back to T-licious.

By now it was late and Sun Haven had grown quiet. The stores had gone dark and the sidewalks were lit only by the orbs of streetlights. The lights were still on in T-licious, but the store was empty and the door was locked. Sean and the Alien Frog Beast must have been in the back, counting the night's take. Kai thought of knocking, then changed his mind. He slid the apartment key through the mail slot and turned away.

He was free. Finally. Each step down the dark sidewalk felt light, as if he were walking on air. It felt good, but edgy and unsettling, too. For the first time in his life he was completely alone in the world. No one was concerned with his whereabouts, or his safety, or his health. From now on it was all on him, and him alone.

He thought briefly about going to the Driftwood and asking Curtis if he could stay there for the night, but he remembered the office was closed and the no vacancy sign meant the motel was full. Instead he headed for the L. Balter & Son funeral home and around to the parking lot in the back. Bean was his best shot at a place to stay that night. But when Kai got to the back of the funeral home, he stopped. In the moonlight he saw a second car parked next to Bean's hearse. It was a black Mercedes-Benz station wagon with California license plates. The same one Kai had seen parked in Spazzy's driveway, the one belonging to Spazzy's older sister. Kai looked up at Bean's apartment on the second floor. The windows were dark.

Kai felt a smile creep across his lips. So that was Bean's non-life-threatening plan. Way to go, dude.

On the other hand, it meant finding another place to stay. Kai walked back down the driveway to Main Street. There was one other possibility. He went down the block and looked up at the apartment over Tuck's Hardware where Jade lived. Dull orange light flickered against the white curtains—inside a candle was burning. He crossed the street, went in the door next to the hardware store, and up the stairs.

The door to Jade's apartment was wooden and green. A crystal hung from a nail at eye level, as if containing some magic protective spell. Kai could hear soft music coming from inside. He touched the bell for an instant.

Murmurs joined the soft music inside the apartment. Jade's voice. Then another voice. Deeper. Male. Kai stepped back from the doorway and a few steps down the stairs, then waited.

"Who is it?" Jade asked from inside.

"Kai. It's nothing. Sorry to bother you. I'm going."

"No, wait."

Kai heard the sound of a bolt sliding open, then the doorknob turned. Jade stuck her head out. She gave him a soft, concerned look. Her black silk robe caught the dim hall light. "Did you need something?"

"No."

Jade gave him a confused look.

"I made a mistake," Kai said.

Jade's eyes darted back into the apartment. Then she looked at Kai again. "Not necessarily."

Kai couldn't help smiling a little. "It's not that. I'm looking for a place to stay tonight."

Jade pursed her lips. "Oh, I'm sorry, Kai."

"I know," Kai said. "Me too. You wouldn't have an old blanket, would you?"

Jade smiled. "You bet. Give me a sec."

Kai waited on the stairs. He caught snippets of conversation from inside the apartment. Whoever the guy was, he didn't sound happy. From the tone of Jade's answers it sounded like she was telling him to chill.

It took longer than Kai expected for Jade to return to the door, and when she did, he saw why. She had a gray blanket for him, but also a large bottle of water and a white plastic grocery bag knotted at the top. "Hope you like ham and cheese," she said, handing it all to him.

"My favorite," said Kai.

"When I was younger, before I had a place of my own, I spent some of the best nights of my life on the beach."

"Thanks," Kai said.

He went back out to the sidewalk and started toward the beach. The moon was a sliver and the stars were out. Kai felt the slight, moist onshore breeze against his face as the ocean-cooled air flooded over the sun-scorched land like a salve. He crossed the boardwalk and for a moment thought about sleeping under it, but then rejected that idea. He wanted to be under the stars.

He walked along the sand toward the Driftwood. There was no sense sleeping in front of the boardwalk where the police or some early riser might disturb him in the morning. This being Sun Haven, there was a law—not always enforced, but a law nonetheless—against sleeping on the beach.

The sand back near the dunes was the

driest, and still held some of the warmth from the day's sunlight. Kai spread Jade's blanket, then lay down and rolled, making a cocoon for himself. Down the beach the ocean's dark waters lapped quietly at the shore. For once Kai was glad there was no surf roaring in his ears. He wiggled a bit to make a comfortable impression in the sand, then lay quietly, gazing up at the stars. A satellite traveled slowly across the sky, growing bright, then dim before disappearing. Shuffled lightly by the breeze, the dune grass made the slightest scratching sounds. Kai felt his eyes grow heavy. He was alone, but not uncomfortable. Not as long as he was on a beach near the ocean.

Six

"**W**hoa, look what washed up during the night," someone said.

Kai opened his eyes. In the dull gray light of the predawn he found Curtis standing over him, holding a familiar square-shaped bottle by the neck. Kai shivered and sat up in his sandy bed. He brushed some grains from his face and pulled Jade's blanket up over his shoulders.

"Sleep well?" Curtis asked.

"Gets a little cold toward morning," Kai said.

Curtis held the bottle out. "Take a hit of this. It'll warm you right up."

Kai accepted the bottle and took a gulp. The whisky burned from the back of his throat all the way down to his stomach, but Kai wasn't sure it made the rest of him actually feel any warmer. He handed the bottle back. "I thought you usually mixed a little coffee into your Jack Daniel's in the morning."

"Is it morning already?" Curtis looked around and pretended to be surprised. "Son of a gun."

"Guess that means you've been up all night, huh?" Kai asked with a yawn.

"Yup." Curtis eased himself down on the sand beside Kai and took a swig of JD. "The harsh light of financial reality has descended upon my feeble domicile, leaving me no chance of respite."

"In English, old man."

"Taxes, grom. Hotel occupancy taxes, sales taxes, real estate taxes, corporate taxes, income taxes. The funds the government must exact from our sorry hides in order to finance such crucial endeavors as invading oil-rich Middle Eastern countries, building space stations, and developing ever more potent weapons of mass destruction. I am proud to admit that I have failed to see the purpose in contributing my allotted share of capital to such insidious activities. Thus I have been judged negligent in my duties as a citizen of this great, but misguided country. In other words . . . I've been a bit lax . . . about paying the tax."

"How much do you owe?" Kai asked.

"Hard to know for sure, grom, what with back taxes, interest, and penalties. But I would imagine I am on the wrong side of high five figures, maybe even six."

Kai let out a low whistle. At least seventy thousand dollars. Maybe as much as ninety thousand dollars. Possibly even more than a hundred thousand. "What can you do?"

Curtis shrugged and took another hit of JD. "Guess I could hole up in one of my upstairs rooms with a box of shotgun shells and shoot it out. Trouble is, it don't seem fair that anyone should get hurt because of my personal politics and financial irresponsibility. Otherwise I guess I'll just have to sell the place, pay what I owe, and paddle off into the sunset."

"No other possibilities?" Kai asked.

Curtis shook his head. "None that come to mind. Although I do have a date to meet with a scaly creature called a tax attorney, which, I have been told, is one of the lower forms of human life, but, like a leech, has been known to be effective in alleviating certain afflictions common to mankind."

While it was often difficult to figure out precisely what Curtis was saying, especially early in the morning, when not all of one's brain cells were actively engaged, it seemed to Kai that this meant that the tax attorney might help the old surfer find a way out of this mess.

They sat together on the sand. This morning the clouds were narrow stripes of pink across the light turquoise blue predawn. As the sun approached from the other side of the horizon the stripes began to glow neon pink. Once again the water was glassy except for the spots here and there where it boiled with bluefish feeding at the surface and seagulls squawking as they picked off hapless prey.

"Amazing, ain't it?" Curtis said. "We're sittin' here taking in this calm mellow beauty of the early morning. The stillness of it. The quiet. The colors. The peacefulness. Unless you happen to be one of those bait fish. Right now for them it's utter mayhem. Chaos. Life and death. No time to stop and smell the roses or whatever it is that bait fish smell. Even on this most beautiful of mornings, it's kill or be killed. Eat or be eaten. Behold, grom, the deceptive beauty and utter viciousness of mother nature. Nothing is spared. As the philosopher once said, 'Time is a great teacher. Unfortunately she kills all of her students.'"

They heard a car and looked down the beach. The yellow Hummer was parked on the far edge of the boardwalk and Buzzy and Lucas were standing beside it, gazing unhappily at the water.

"All bow to the king and crown prince," Curtis whispered.

Buzzy and Lucas climbed back into the Hummer. The doors slammed and they drove away.

"You think he had anything to do with it?" Kai asked.

"My tax problems?" Curtis shook his head. "No. This is one mess I got myself into with no outside help, grom. Buzzy Frank is blameless, at least as far as this one's concerned."

"What happened between you two, anyway?" asked Kai.

"Now there's a question," Curtis replied. He took another hit of Jack Daniel's and shivered as it went down. "I've thought a lot about it myself, and I suppose it comes down to human nature. Down to what is, versus what isn't, but craves to be. Take basic board skills and natural ability. I had 'em, grom. Was born with 'em. Took 'em for granted. Surfed for fun and hardly ever practiced anything. Buzzy on the other hand never had it. Had to work for it. And I mean work hard. I'd see someone do something new on a wave, and on the next wave I'd do it too. Buzzy would have to practice it over and over again. Day after day. Week after week. You can see how that might make him a little bit resentful."

Kai nodded. "And why he might push Lucas so hard."

"Oh, yeah. For Buzzy everything is work. Everything is discipline. He got used to it. He got good at it. He's reaped the rewards of hard work. Now he's about as rich and powerful as they come around here. Me, I never cared for work. Never cared for discipline. Just took each day as it came and tried to find something of value in it."

"Which way do you think is better?" Kai asked.

Curtis raised his eyebrows in surprise. "Neither. There's no better. No worse. It's just life. It may look like Buzzy Frank's got everything a man could want, but if that was the case then why's he still working so hard to get more?"

"Because maybe he's wrong," Kai said. "Maybe he just thinks this is what he wants, but it really isn't."

"Could be," Curtis said. "Or maybe he's right. Maybe this is exactly what he needs, and if he doesn't get it then he's *really* a miserable son of a bitch."

"Seems pretty miserable already," Kai said.

"That may be his lot in life. To be rich, powerful, and miserable. He wouldn't be the first."

"And what's your lot in life?" Kai asked.

"To be poor, powerless, and miserable." Curtis grinned, then took another gulp of JD. "And drunk. At least, most of the time."

"Can't people change?"

"I don't know," Curtis answered. "I've been waitin' all my life for the answer to that one. I'm still waitin' to find out."

Thirty yards offshore a bluefish leaped clear out of the water, then splashed back down.

"So tell me, grom, what brings you to lay your weary head down on the cool sands of Sun Haven beach?"

"I can't take my father's scams anymore," Kai said.

"Over at the T-shirt shop?"

"Only now it's the discount surfwear and T-shirt shop," Kai corrected him, "where he's selling cheap knockoffs of all the name brands."

"No kidding?" Curtis said. "Seems to me that would be a serious violation of the laws that govern polite society. Your father certainly is an enterprising fellow, isn't he?"

"Except his greatest joy in life is ripping everyone off," Kai said.

"So you chose to make an exit, or did he leave you no choice?"

"It was mutual."

"How old are you, grom?"

"Fifteen."

"Fifteen and on your own. Well, you're a capable enough young man from what I've seen. Still workin' for Teddy?"

"Yeah, but I'm not making any money," Kai said. "I'm still paying off the board she gave me."

"She know about this?" Curtis nodded at the impression in the sand Kai had made during the night.

51

"No. It just happened last night. You're the only one who knows."

Curtis twisted his head around and looked back up the beach. "You sure about that, grom?"

Jade, wearing shorts and a loose-fitting T-shirt, was coming toward them carrying two large white paper cups.

"Thought you might need this," she said, handing Kai a cup covered with a white plastic top. The cup was hot and Kai could smell the coffee.

"Thanks, Jade. You know Curtis?" Kai asked. "He owns the Driftwood Motel."

"Hi," Jade said.

"Jade works at Sun Haven Surf," Kai told Curtis.

Curtis offered her his hand and they shook. "We've seen each other around town."

"You want this one?" Jade asked, gesturing to the other coffee cup.

"No, thanks." Curtis got up from the sand. "I've got a full motel for once. I should probably get back to the office before too many of my current guests take leave without settling their motel bills. You take care of this young man, okay?"

"I'll try," Jade said.

"I know you like sleeping on the beach," Curtis said to Kai, "but the bedbugs at my place get ornery if they don't get fed regular. You need a place to stay tonight, you know where to come."

"Thanks, old man," Kai said.

"No sweat." Curtis limped away, clutching the neck of the Jack Daniel's bottle.

"Kind of early to start drinking, isn't it?" Jade asked Kai in a low voice.

"He's still going from last night," Kai said. "I don't think it's morning yet as far as he's concerned." He took a sip of coffee. "This is really great. Thanks for bringing it down. What about your friend?"

Jade shrugged. "Another possessive loser."

"Look at it this way," Kai said. "They wouldn't be possessive unless they thought you were worth possessing."

"Sometimes I think I wouldn't mind being possessed. Only it would have to be by the right guy." Jade looked back up the beach as if she knew she had to get back. She sighed. "He'll probably be waking up soon and will get all freaked out if I'm not there. Guess I better go."

"Wait." Kai got to his feet and shook out the blanket, then folded it. "Normally I'd wash it before I gave it back, but I don't have access to a washing machine."

"It's okay." Jade took the blanket. "I appreciate the thought. Sure you won't need it again tonight?"

"Don't know," Kai said. They started to walk up the beach together.

"Then maybe you ought to keep it."

"How about, if I need it I'll let you know?" Jade gave him a curious look.

"There is something else, though," Kai said. "Sort of a big favor."

"Okay."

"How long have you been working at the surf shop?"

Jade frowned as if this wasn't what she'd expected him to ask. "A couple of years, why?"

"Long enough to have noticed that Big Dave doesn't like Buzzy very much?"

"I don't think he can stand Buzzy," Jade said. "Like he almost hates him."

"So why does he keep working there?" Kai asked.

"Are you kidding?" Jade said. "Dave McAllister's the chairman of the boardroom.

The big Kahuna. Hero to all the little grem-mies. If he didn't have that job he'd be work-ing in McDonald's."

"Only there are no McDonald's in Sun Haven," Kai said.

"Exactly," said Jade.

"So how well do you know Big Dave?"

Jade groaned. "Too well. I mean, not that anything's ever happened between us. But not a day goes by that he doesn't let me know how much he wishes something *would* happen."

"So this favor I need to ask," Kai said. "It's not really for me, but for someone else."

"And it involves me being nice to Dave?" Jade guessed.

"You got it."

Jade took a deep breath and let it out slowly and reluctantly. "How important is this?"

"Big-time, Jade. I mean, huge. Think you could do it?"

"You haven't told me what it is," Jade said. "Do I have to get him to do something?"

"No, you just have to get him to tell you something. A secret."

Jade smiled. "That's all?"

"It could be a big secret," Kai warned. "One

he might not be willing to tell without some, er, encouragement."

"If it's really that important, I'll see what I can do."

"Thanks, Jade."

Seven

Kai headed over to Teddy's. Now that he was helping her shape and glass boards, there was usually work for him whenever he had the time. And it looked like from now on he'd have plenty of time. He walked along the high white picket fence in front of her house and turned the corner.

Buzzy Frank's yellow Hummer was parked at the curb. Kai stopped for a moment, uncertain of whether he should go in. Suddenly he heard a loud voice coming through an open window in Teddy's backyard shop.

"I don't care what you do, Buzzy." Teddy sounded angry. "There is no way that is ever going to happen."

"Don't be stupid, Teddy," Buzzy shot back. "Almost all your business comes through my store."

"That's correct, Buzzy, and you take a very handsome commission for that," Teddy replied. "An incredibly handsome commission considering all you do is write down an order on a piece of paper. I do all the rest. So I think that the money you get for that should be more than enough to make you very happy."

"It's not about the money," Buzzy said.

"Oh, cut the crap," Teddy snapped. "It's *always* about money, and you and I both know it. It's about building a Sun Haven Surf brand to compete against Hobie and Rusty and CI. Next thing I know, you'll have a warehouse full of shapers pumping out Sun Haven boards. Or maybe I'm giving you too much credit. Why pay shapers when you can churn out machine-made garbage?"

"You'd be my top designer, Teddy," Buzzy said. "You could design all day instead of wasting your time shaping and glassing. Whose name is on every Channel Islands board? Merrick's. It's the same with Rusty and all the rest of them. Picture it, Teddy.

Your name on thousands of boards all over the world."

"Did it ever occur to you that maybe I like shaping and glassing my own boards?" Teddy asked. "That maybe I take pride in my work and the only way I can ensure that it meets my standards is by being hands-on with every single one?"

"Then it's time you woke up, Teddy," Buzzy said. "Ten years from now there'll hardly be any hand-shaped boards at all. Everything will be done by computer-guided grinding machines, precise to less than a milli-meter. It's going the way of cars, Teddy. All computer robotics. There'll be no tolerance for the kind of errors that shapers make. Hand-shaped boards are the Ghost of Surfing Past."

"Then I prefer the past," Teddy spit. "Truth be known I don't particularly care for the present and I sure as hell don't like what I'm hearing about the future. Now I believe our business here is finished. If I were you, I'd get into that big yellow armored car of yours and go back to your shop and count all that money that you probably don't have any idea what to do with."

"You're making a mistake, Teddy."

"And you're making me mad."

"There are plenty of other shapers around."

"Get out of my workshop, mister."

The door to the workshop opened and Buzzy came out. Kai pretended he was only now turning the corner and coming down the sidewalk. As Buzzy let himself out the driveway gate, he saw Kai. They both stopped.

"I know what your father's up to," Buzzy said. "It won't be pretty when the ax comes down on him."

"That the same ax that came down on Curtis's boards or a different one?" Kai asked.

"That was a butter knife compared to this," Buzzy said. "This'll be a guillotine."

Kai knew from experience that his father had no intention of being anywhere near Sun Haven when the ax or guillotine came down. The Alien Frog Beast planned to be two thousand miles away with a new name, a new driver's license, and a new store. The only thing he'd be missing was his younger son.

Lucas's father still hadn't moved. Kai couldn't imagine why.

"That was a nice ride you had over in Fairport," Buzzy finally said.

"Thanks."

"Lucas says you might compete in the Northeast Championship here in a few weeks," Lucas's father said.

"Might."

"I hope you will. It would be good for him. He needs someone to light a fire under him."

"You never know," Kai said, thinking back to the Fourth of July. "It might explode in his face."

Buzzy's features hardened. Without a word he got into the Hummer and drove away. Kai went through the gate and knocked on the door to Teddy's workshop.

She didn't answer. That was strange. Kai knew she was in there. Maybe she'd gone into the shaping room and couldn't hear him. He knocked again. This time a little louder.

"Go away."

"Teddy, it's me, Kai."

"So? What part of the sentence didn't you understand? 'Go'? Or 'away'?"

"Come on, Teddy."

She didn't answer.

"Teddy?" Kai tried again.

"Get away from my workshop."

"You already used that line," Kai reminded her. "Or at least something pretty close to it."

Again Teddy was silent.

"Look, Teddy, I admire what you said to Buzzy. The guy's a cold-blooded bastard. But it's hard to go up against someone like that alone. We all need friends and I'm one of yours. So how about it?"

"Oh, all right, come in."

Kai pushed the door open. Teddy was sitting on a stool by the workbench, a defeated slope to her shoulders as she stared at the floor. She was a small woman, but today she looked even smaller.

"I guess it's obvious that I heard part of that conversation with Buzzy," Kai said.

"Greedy, power-hungry son of a bitch," Teddy muttered.

"I didn't quite get what he wanted," Kai said. "Your boards with a Sun Haven Surf brand logo on them?"

Teddy swept her arm around the workshop. "This is my life. It may not seem like much, but it's all I've got and it's the only thing I do. I make the best boards I can, and every surfer around here knows that when they see a plain white board with the handwritten letters *TL* on the stringer it came from this shop and these hands."

"Then don't let him do it," Kai said.

"How can I stop him?" Teddy asked. "You and I both know that almost all my business comes from orders he takes at the store. The custom boards, the repairs . . . All that work comes from Sun Haven Surf."

"Open your own business," Kai said. "Custom-shaped boards and ding repairs. You've got a shop. All you'd have to do is advertise in the local paper."

"You think I'd let *strangers* come in here?" Teddy asked. "Wander all over my property? Are you crazy?"

"Then maybe you could rent a small place in town," Kai said. "It would cost you more, but you'd probably get more business. Walk-ins and stuff."

Teddy gave him a curious look. "How does a kid your age know about this?"

"It's what I've been doing for the past two years," Kai said.

Teddy blinked. "Oh, right, with your father. Wait a minute. What are you doing here? You work for him during the day."

"Not anymore," Kai said.

"What happened?"

"He's a crook," Kai said. "I got to the point where I couldn't take it."

"So I'm not the only one who's out of a job right now," Teddy realized.

"You could say that."

"And you think you learned about business from him?"

"Kind of a mixture of what to do and what not to do," Kai said. "By watching him do it wrong, I hope I figured out what was right."

"Then, we'd be partners in this venture?" Teddy asked with an amused expression.

"However you want to do it," Kai said.

Teddy smiled and shook her head. "You're good, you know that? For a second there you almost made a believer out of me. How old are you? Seventeen?"

"Fifteen," Kai said.

Teddy slapped her own cheek gently, as if to wake herself up from a dream. "Hello? Anyone home? Am I really listening to a fifteen-year-old tell me to go into business for myself? Oh, wait, not for myself. He and I will be partners in our very own surf shop, competing against Buzzy Frank and Sun Haven

Surf. I'm sure Buzzy would be delighted. We'd have his blessings." She pointed at the door to the shaping room. "There's the shaping room. Get to work."

Kai knew better than to argue.

Eight

"**D**udes, this is most definitely the life," Booger said. He was lying on his back on the raft floating in the pool in Spazzy's backyard. On his bare stomach was a slice of pizza, and in his hand was a can of Mountain Dew. It was dark, and the lights around the pool were on, as well as one big underwater spotlight that made the chlorinated water glow aqua blue.

Spazzy, Bean, Everett, and Kai sat at the glass patio table, eating pizza. A couple of evenings a week now, they hung out at Spazzy's house, usually by the pool, or sometimes in the game room, where Jillian and Spazzy had Foosball, air hockey, and Ping-Pong. Jillian was always cool about ordering some pizzas for them, and even after the sun went down, they could hang around the pool as late as they liked.

At that moment Bean was glaring unhappily at Kai. "When?"

"Later," Kai replied.

"What are you talking about?" Spazzy asked.

"Nothing important," Kai said, and gave Bean a look.

"Okay," Spazzy said, and jerked his head toward the house. "What are *they* talking about?"

Kai and the others turned and looked. Through the large glass sliding doors they could see into the kitchen, where Shauna and Jillian were talking. Both were wearing bathing suits and sweatshirts. Shauna's sweatshirt was blue with a hood hanging down the back. Jillian's was green with a zipper in the front.

"Girls can talk forever," Bean said with a shrug.

"Hey, you guys hear about the Northeast Open Surfing Championship?" Spazzy asked. "Like with real prize money and everything?"

Kai and the others nodded.

"You're all entering, right?" Spazzy asked.

"I'm thinking about it," Bean said.

Spazzy twitched and blinked. "What about you, Kai?"

Kai shrugged.

"Wow, I would have thought you'd be totally stoked about this," Spazzy said. "I mean, not just because it's real money, but because it's like a total shot at the big time."

"Don't forget you're not the only person who feels that way," Bean said. "Every kook within five hundred miles is thinking the same thing."

"So?"

"This isn't gonna be a local deal like the Fairport contest," Kai explained. "This is bigtime, with money, which means you're gonna see pros out there. Or, at least, *almost* pros. It's gonna be a whole different level of competition."

"But you gotta try, right?" Spazzy said. "I mean, you guys know Screamers as well as anyone by now."

The sliding door from the house opened, and Jillian and Shauna came out. Jillian sat down next to Bean and gave him a relaxed kiss on the cheek. It was hard to believe that this was the same person who, a month ago, stood by the window, her arms crossed tightly and a frown on her face while she watched Spazzy protectively.

"Have a slice?" Bean pulled the pizza box toward them.

"Okay." Jillian reached in. She folded a slice carefully in half, and then raised it to her mouth and took a dainty bite.

A slight breeze brought a wind chime to life, and one by one Kai and the others turned hopefully to gaze at the dark dunes and the ocean beyond them. After the long stretch of flat days in early August, there'd been a week of knee-highs and ankle-slappers, and now once again, it was almost flat. Perhaps this breeze was the first sign of a change in the weather. Or maybe it was just a flirtatious tease.

"Forget the Northeast Championship," Everett said. "If we don't get some waves soon, we're gonna forget how to surf."

"I guess the only good news is that it's the same up and down the east coast," Booger said, sliding off the raft and climbing up the ladder from the pool.

"It kills me," Bean groaned. "The whole season's five months long at best, and right in the middle of it we always get these doldrums."

"Doldrums?" Booger repeated uncertainly as he toweled off.

"A state of inactivity or stagnation," Jillian said. "Although originally it was used to describe the area of calm between the trade winds."

For a moment everyone stared at her.

"It was an SAT word," Jillian said defensively.

"Hey, it's totally cool," Bean said. "Personally, I think smart is sexy." He started to rise from his chair. "Anyone feel like Ping-Pong?"

"I do," Jillian said.

They headed toward the game room.

"Anyone for air hockey?" Booger asked.

"Yeah," said Everett.

Booger turned to Shauna, Kai, and Spazzy. "How about you guys?"

"I'm cool here," Spazzy said.

"I haven't had a slice yet, so I'm going to eat first," said Shauna. "Then I'll come down."

"I'm gonna hang here too," said Kai.

"Okay." Booger and Everett followed Bean and Jillian through the sliding glass doors toward the game room, leaving Shauna, Kai, and Spazzy alone around the outdoor table.

Spazzy got up. "I gotta take a leak. Be right back."

He went into the house, leaving Shauna and Kai at the table. The light wind made Shauna's hair flutter. It may have been Kai's imagination, but it seemed as though the breeze was growing stronger, which might be a good thing if it brought swells with it.

"Jillian wants to have a party for Spazzy," Shauna said. "Before they go back to California."

"That what you guys were talking about?" Kai asked.

She nodded.

"Sounds like a great idea," said Kai.

"I told her I thought she might want to invite Lucas and his friends," Shauna said.

Kai gazed at her, surprised. "Why?"

"Well, Jillian and Spazzy are going to come back next summer, and I thought it would be nice if Lucas and his friends understood Spazzy better," Shauna explained. "So that if he wants to surf Screamers and you're not . . ." Her words trailed off.

"Here?" Kai filled in the blank for her.

Shauna nodded.

A napkin blew off the table and onto the

ground. Kai reached down and picked it up. The slightest trace of fall was in the air. It was impossible to imagine where he'd be next summer. To be honest, it wasn't easy to imagine where he'd be next month.

"It's a nice idea," Kai said. "I just don't see Lucas going for it."

"You never know," Shauna said.

They sat quietly after that. Kai gazed up at the night sky dotted with stars. A few thin gray clouds drifted overhead, but the sky was mostly clear. Without warning, a thin bright beam of light streaked parallel to the horizon and vanished.

Kai looked at Shauna. "Did you see that?"

She nodded. "Was it a shooting star?"

"I think so."

"I've never actually seen one before," Shauna said. "Have you?"

"In Hawaii a few times," Kai said.

"What's Hawaii like?" Shauna asked.

"It's the best place on Earth." Kai smiled. "I mean, I don't know much about what it's like on the big island or on Maui. But Kauai . . . Hanalei . . . It's just the best."

"You really miss it?"

Kai nodded. He missed it terribly, except

for one memory so bad that he still wasn't sure he could ever go back.

"And that's where you saw shooting stars?" Shauna asked.

"Yeah. The sky there is much darker. You see tons more stars and they really shimmer. I guess it's because there aren't as many lights around. Sometimes at night my mom and I would put out lounges in the front yard and lie on them and look up."

"Let's do it." Shauna nodded at a pair of lounges by the pool. She and Kai moved over to them and laid back with their faces tilted up at the sky. The breeze came up again and sent the slightest chill across Kai's bare skin.

"Kai, what happened to your mom?" Shauna asked from the lounge beside him.

"I told you. She got killed in a car accident."

"But there's more, isn't there?"

Kai gazed over at her, wondering how she knew. "Yeah."

"You don't have to tell me," Shauna said. "Unless you want to."

He looked up at the night sky again. He'd never told anyone. The only people who knew were those who'd been there that day, or who'd read about it in the newspaper on Kauai.

"I used to think I was really hot stuff," Kai said.

"As a surfer?"

"Right. You think Buzzy Frank is competitive? You should have seen me."

"I don't believe that," Shauna said.

"You think Sam is a jerk about being a local and trying to keep everyone off Screamers? He isn't half the jerk I was."

"Kai, that can't be true," Shauna said.

"Believe it," Kai said.

"Believe what?" Spazzy asked, coming back outside.

Neither Kai nor Shauna answered.

"Uh-oh, another big secret." Spazzy started to twitch. "I'll go back inside and leave you two alone."

"No, it's okay," Shauna said. "Guess what? We just saw a shooting star."

Spazzy pointed a finger toward the horizon. "Out over there, right?"

"You saw it, too?" Shauna asked.

"No, but that's where the constellation Perseus is, and that's where most of the shooting stars come from at this time of year."

"But they're not really stars," Shauna said. "They're just meteors."

"Not even," said Spazzy. "Most of them are particles of dust. No bigger than a grain of sand." He looked around. "If you really want to see them, let's go down to the beach and away from the lights around the pool."

Shauna and Kai got up and went across the walkway through the dunes with Spazzy, who explained that the shooting stars were mostly particles of dust left in the trail of the comet Swift–Tuttle. "Every summer around now, the earth's orbit passes through this huge dust cloud left by the comet, and we get these meteor showers called the Perseids because it looks like they come from around that constellation."

"I always thought meteors traveled through space and burned up when they went through the atmosphere," Shauna said.

"Well, maybe some do," Spazzy replied. "But most of the shooting stars we see are tiny particles just hanging in space. They don't come to us. We go to them."

"I never knew that," Shauna said.

"Yeah, it's amazing how much junk you can learn when you don't have any friends," Spazzy said.

They got down to the beach and sat in the sand looking out at the horizon.

"Know what, Spazzy?" Kai said. "It's actually pretty cool that you and your sister know all this stuff. Maybe it wasn't much fun learning, but at least you know it. I mean, face it, in the long run, what's more important? Knowing where shooting stars come from or knowing how to party?"

"Knowing how to party," Spazzy and Shauna answered at the same time, and then laughed.

"Yeah, yeah." Kai grinned. Then he heard a sound that had grown scarce over the past week—the splash of a wave. Spazzy and Shauna stopped laughing. Kai knew they'd heard it too. All three of them turned their gazes to the water's edge where a small set of ankle-slappers were tumbling onto the sand.

"Could be the beginning of something," Spazzy said.

"Keep your fingers crossed," said Shauna.

Kai glanced at his watch. It was later than he thought. Time for Bean and him to go.

"I gotta book, folks." He started to get up.

Spazzy frowned. "Where?"

"Just something Bean and I have to take care of," Kai said. "No biggie."

"Yeah, okay." Spazzy and Shauna got up

with him, and they went back to the house and into the game room. The loud clatter of air hockey and the pock of a Ping-Pong ball met their ears before they reached the bottom of the stairs. The room felt warm and smelled faintly of sweat. Over by the air hockey table both Booger and Everett were bare chested, their foreheads speckled with perspiration.

"Hey, Kai," Booger said. "Want to play the winner?"

"Thanks, dude, I would," Kai said, "but Bean and I have somewhere to go."

Bean checked his watch, registering surprise that the time had already come. Jillian frowned.

"Go somewhere now?" she asked, more of Bean than Kai.

"It's okay," Bean said.

"Just you two?" asked Booger.

Kai nodded. He'd hoped he and Bean could just slip away. He hadn't meant to make it seem like such a big deal.

"Is something wrong?" Jillian asked, and Kai knew at once that she was more than just book smart.

"It's okay," Bean assured her. "I'll call you tomorrow."

They went outside and got into the hearse.

"Why can't we just tell the police that Goldilocks has the boards and we think they belong to Curtis and they're stolen?" Bean asked as he turned the key in the ignition.

"Bean, if someone stole your surfboard and you found it, could you prove it was yours?" Kai asked.

"Yeah, because I wrote down the serial number," Bean said, steering the hearse out onto the dark street.

"Right. But suppose you didn't write down that number. *Then* could you prove it? Do you have any paperwork? A receipt?"

"No. Who keeps a receipt for a surfboard?"

"Exactly. Now the problem with Curtis is he never wrote down the serial numbers. Everyone knows they're his boards, but no one can prove it."

"Why do we have to be the ones to get them back?" Bean asked.

"Because it's the right thing to do," said Kai.

"Why can't we let someone else do the right thing?"

"You're joking?" Kai asked.

"Yeah, yeah, I know," Bean said with a sigh. "We're the ones who have to do the right thing because there is no one else."

They drove quietly for a while, then Bean said, "You see how Jillian knew right away that something was up?"

"Sorry about that," Kai said.

"It's cool," Bean said. "I just don't want her to start thinking you're a bad influence on me, you know?"

They both grinned. It was kind of funny to think that Kai, at the age of fifteen, could be a bad influence on Bean, who was nineteen.

"Maybe I am," Kai said.

"No," said Bean. "Just different. And good, if you want to know the truth. Only it'll be a lot better once this night is over."

"I won't argue with that," Kai said.

Nine

Bean pulled onto Seaside Drive and headed for Belle Harbor.

"You sure you remember the way?" he asked.

"Pretty much," Kai said. "We pass 88s and make the first left after the train tracks. It's the road with the sod farm on the left and the woods on the right."

"That much I remember," Bean said. "But then he made us put those bandannas over our eyes. It's where we go after that that I'm asking about."

"I'll let you know when we get there," Kai said.

Bean gnawed nervously on the side of his

thumb. "Know what's gonna happen if he catches us?"

"First of all he's not gonna catch us," Kai said. "And second, even if he did, what would he do? Go to the police?"

"I was thinking more along the lines of baseball bats," Bean said.

"He doesn't strike me as the type," Kai said.

Bean turned to him with a raised eyebrow. "How would you know? You have any experience with anyone who *would* strike you as the type?"

Kai didn't answer. There'd been some people along the way. "Associates" of his father's, who were probably pretty handy with baseball bats and not in any way that involved a ball. Not to mention those guys with the bulges under their shirts, who hung around the warehouse in Brooklyn.

"Ever try to run and swing a bat at the same time?" Kai asked.

"No," said Bean.

"It's not easy."

"What if there's no place to run?" Bean asked.

"Then you duck."

They passed 88s. By this time of night the

parking lot was almost full, and the dance club was brightly lit.

Ahead, in the hearse's headlights, they saw the yellow railroad crossing sign. A moment later the hearse bounced over the tracks. Bean turned left onto the narrow paved road between the sod farm and the woods. Kai closed his eyes and started to count.

"What are you doing?" Bean asked.

"Shush."

Kai counted up to twenty-five. "There's gonna be a right turn coming up."

"Yeah, I see it," Bean said.

Kai opened his eyes just as Bean turned onto a dirt road that went into the woods.

"What next?" Bean asked.

"Quiet." Kai closed his eyes and counted as they bounced down the dirt road. This time he counted to fifteen. "Left turn."

"Yup, there it is," said Bean.

They turned left. Kai closed his eyes and counted to twenty. "Okay, stop." He opened his eyes. The dirt road was hardly wide enough for the hearse.

"This it?" Bean asked.

"Not quite," Kai said. "Where's the flashlight?"

"Behind you."

Kai reached behind the seat and came up with a heavy-duty flashlight—the kind that ran off a nine-volt battery. It was just what he'd hoped for. He rolled down the passenger-side window and turned the flashlight on.

"Okay, let's go nice and slow." Kai aimed the flashlight into the woods. Bean drove slowly. The dirt road was full of bumps and potholes and the hearse creaked and squeaked as it lumbered along.

"You can see why Goldilocks prefers a Jeep," Bean said.

A small pair of emerald green eyes glittered at them from the dark. A possum. Bean practically came to a stop to give the sluggish creature time to get out of the way.

"You've heard of guard dogs?" he asked. "There's a guard possum."

Kai kept scanning the woods with the flashlight. "No offense, Bean, but was that supposed to be funny?"

"Just nervous babbling," Bean admitted.

"I'm telling you, dude, there's nothing to be nervous about," said Kai.

They drove a little farther. Kai swept the beam through the woods, looking for the shed.

"You sure we're on the right road?" Bean asked.

"Pretty sure," Kai answered.

"Seems like we should have found it by now."

"Don't forget, last time we came down this road a lot faster," Kai said. "So it may seem like we've been driving longer, but it's only because we're going slower. There it is." Kai held the beam steady on the shed, just barely visible through the trees. "Get as close as you can and stop."

A few seconds later Bean stopped the hearse. "You know, something just occurred to me. Up till now I've been worried that Goldilocks was gonna nail us while we were stealing his boards."

"We're not stealing," Kai said. "We're simply returning the boards to their rightful owner."

"Yeah, okay, Robin Hood, whatever," Bean said. "But here's what I just realized. It doesn't matter whether he catches us in the act or not, because as soon as he discovers the boards are gone, he's gonna know who took them."

"Not necessarily," Kai said. "We don't know who else he's shown the boards to. Now come on, let's do this fast and get out of here.

You have the hacksaw and the WD-Forty?"

"Of course," Bean said. They got out of the hearse. Bean opened the back door and took out the hacksaw and spray can of oil. He and Kai walked through the dark trees toward the shed.

"I understand the hacksaw, but what's the oil for?" Bean asked.

"Cuts down on the noise the saw makes going through metal," Kai said.

"Sometimes you scare me," Bean said as they made their way around the tree trunks and through the brush.

"Why's that?" Kai asked.

"Because when most people use a hacksaw, they don't have to worry about how much noise it makes. The only people who have to worry about noise are the ones who are doing something where they don't want to get caught. Know what I mean? So tell me Kai, where'd you learn this little trick?"

Kai knew exactly where he'd learned to make a hacksaw work silently. About a year before, a store his father had been using was suddenly bolted shut by the landlord for non-payment of rent. It was one of those rare times when Pat had failed to leave town before the landlord figured out that he was getting stiffed. Since the store was padlocked with all the shirts, transfers, heat press, and computer still inside, the Alien Frog Beast had had no choice but to break in during the night. The only other option would have been to pay the rent he owed. Which, of course, was out of the question.

"Just something I picked up along the way," Kai said, taking the hacksaw from Bean and handing him the flashlight. "Shine it on the latch."

Bean aimed the flashlight. Kai had no intention of trying to saw through the padlock itself. That was case-hardened steel. It was the latch he was interested in. Especially where it crossed the gap between the old wooden doors. Kai placed the blade of the hacksaw on the latch and started to saw.

"Give it a shot," he said when the metal screeched. "Just a little."

Bean sprayed the oil, and continued to apply it each time the saw began to make noise. Kai sawed steadily. The latch was old and the metal soft. In less than five minutes he'd cut through it. He and Bean pulled open the doors. Bean flashed the light on the boards and Kai quickly counted. All twelve were still there. Kai felt himself smile. Except for the banana yellow Yater, Curtis was going to get his boards back.

They carefully pulled the boards out of the shed and piled them into the back of the hearse, using towels and wet suits and anything else soft to keep them from banging against each other. When they were finished they pushed the shed doors closed and propped some large rocks against them.

"Got any duct tape?" Kai asked.

Bean went back to the hearse and got the roll he always kept. He gave it to Kai, who carefully taped the back of the latch together so it wouldn't be immediately obvious that someone had broken in.

"Smart," Bean said as they walked back to the hearse. "So if Goldilocks drives by just to check, it'll look like everything's okay."

"If we're lucky," Kai said.

They got into the hearse and headed back out the dirt road. A few minutes later they turned onto Seaside Drive, went over the railroad tracks, and drove toward Sun Haven. Bean let out a loud sigh. "Man, am I glad that's over."

"Me too." Kai peered into the side-view

mirror. Far in the distance behind them, a pair of headlights appeared.

"I assume we're going to the Driftwood to drop the boards off," Bean said.

"Not exactly." The headlights behind them were growing larger. Whoever was driving the car was in a rush. Kai decided he was just being paranoid. Seaside Drive was a pretty heavily traveled road, and it could have been anyone.

"Not exactly?" Bean repeated. "Where are we taking them if not to Curtis?"

"I'll let you know," Kai said, trying not to sound distracted, but the headlights had now caught up to them. He resisted the urge to turn around and look through the back window. With the hearse curtain in place it would be impossible to see anyway. Seaside Drive was empty, and the dashed white line down the center of the road allowed the car behind them to pass if the driver wanted to.

Only the driver didn't want to. Instead he stayed behind the hearse. Kai reminded himself again that it could be anyone, and there were a thousand reasons why the driver might decide not to pass. They were coming to an intersection with a traffic light. The light was green.

"Do me a favor?" Kai said. "Put on your left blinker and slow down as if you're going to make a turn."

Bean instantly looked into the rearview mirror. "Why? We're not turning, are we?"

"No."

"Then?"

"Just do it."

Bean flicked on the blinker and started to slow down. The car behind them put on its blinker. They were almost at the intersection.

"Want me to turn?" Bean asked.

"No. Speed up and go straight."

Bean sped up, and looked in the rearview mirror. Instead of turning, the car behind them did the same thing.

"Shit," Bean muttered. Now he understood.

"Next intersection act like you're driving through and then quickly make a right," Kai said.

"As long as it's not a dead end," Bean added.

"Correct."

The next intersection had four-way stop signs. Bean stopped, looked around, then accelerated as if he were going straight, only to hang a last-minute screeching right. Kai winced at the sound of the boards in the back clunking into one another. He hated the thought of dinging them. The car behind them suddenly hung a right too.

"Please be a cop," Bean muttered, looking into the side-view mirror. "Please be a cop."

"Don't think so," said Kai.

"Red Jeep?"

"Not that either."

"Then maybe it's someone we don't know," Bean said hopefully.

"Or it's Goldilocks with a friend," said Kai.

Bean groaned loudly and kept driving through the dark.

"Any idea where this road goes?" Kai asked.

"Not a clue," Bean said. He started to chew on the side of his thumb again. "I'm not happy. I'm really not happy. I'm *extremely* not happy."

Kai had an idea. "He once called you on your cell phone, right?"

"Yeah? So?"

"Don't cell phones usually save the return numbers?"

Bean glanced at Kai. "Are you crazy?"

Kai pointed at the car behind them. "You

know a better way to find out if that's him?"

"You really are crazy," Bean said.

"What's the problem?"

It was Bean's turn to gesture to the car following them. "What if it *is* him?"

"Then he already knows where we are, so what do we have to lose?"

"I hope you know what you're doing." Bean dug his cell phone out of his pocket, and handed it to Kai, who went through the numbers, reading the names out loud until he got to Albert Hines.

"Never heard of that one," Bean said. "Could be him."

Kai pressed "send." The phone rang, then someone answered. "Yeah?"

"Albert, that you?" Kai said.

"Yeah, who's this?"

"Where are you right now?" Kai asked.

There was silence for a moment, then Kai heard Goldilocks mutter to himself, "No fricken way."

"You're at No Fricken Way?" Kai asked.

"This the shrooms kid?" Goldilocks asked.

"That's me."

"You got my boards in that hearse?" Goldilocks asked.

"Guess that's you behind us," Kai said.

"Fuck you." Goldilocks hung up.

"It's him?" Bean gestured at the rearview mirror.

"Appears that way," said Kai.

"I don't believe this," Bean moaned.

They were headed down a narrow, winding, tree-lined road. No street lights. Just the thick trunks of trees on both sides. Here and there something streaked in the headlights as a toad hopped away and vanished into the weeds along the sides of the road.

"Don't try to talk me into losing them, okay?" Bean pleaded. "This ain't the movies. I'm not into high-speed chases."

"My guess is, neither are they," Kai said.

In the headlights a sign came into view:

PRIVATE ROAD

BELLE HARBOR GOLF AND TENNIS CLUB

NO TRESPASSING

"Crap," Bean muttered. "Now what do we do?"

"Keep going," said Kai.

Ten

The road was still lined with trees, but instead of weeds and brush, the shoulders were marked with large painted white stones and neatly mowed grass. It was clear they'd entered the grounds of a private country club. The headlights of the second car lit up the hearse's side-view mirrors.

"Do we have any idea what we're doing?" Bean asked.

"Nope," answered Kai.

They bounced over a speed bump, then passed a small, empty guard's station on the right. It was hard to see in the dark, but there appeared to be an empty parking lot on the left. The road ahead led to a large clubhouse. On the right were tennis courts.

The second car stayed behind them. Bean's cell phone rang. Kai looked at the incoming number. "It's him." He pressed the phone to his ear. "Hey, Albert, enjoying the ride?"

"You're trapped," Goldilocks said.

"How's that?"

"The only way out is the way you came in."

"Thanks for telling me," Kai said.

"You ready to get the shit kicked out of you?"

"By anyone I know?" Kai asked.

"It ain't gonna be so funny when you're spitting teeth."

"Hey, that's a good line, Albert," Kai said. "You're getting better."

"I'm gonna enjoy this." Once again Goldilocks hung up.

"What'd he say?" Bean asked nervously.

"He said he's gonna enjoy this."

"Enjoy what?"

"Nothing important."

"We have to do something, Kai," Bean said.

"I know." Kai peered through the windshield. Ahead was the clubhouse.

"Come on, dude," Bean said anxiously, "we're running out of room."

In front of the clubhouse was a round plot of lawn with a tall white statue fountain. The driveway circled the statue then rejoined the drive they were now on.

"Keep going," Kai said.

"I gotcha," Bean said. "If they follow us, we'll both go around and then head back out the way we came."

"Exactly," Kai said.

Bean entered the circular part of the driveway and naturally headed to the right. The car behind them also entered the circular part. Only they headed left. Which meant both cars would meet head on in front of the clubhouse.

"Great idea, Kai," Bean muttered.

"There." Kai pointed through the windshield. "See that road?"

Bean squinted. Barely visible in the dark was a slight turnoff to the right. "No. I don't see any road. I see a path, like for a golf cart or something.."

"Take it," Kai said.

"Are you crazy?" Bean said. "We have no idea where it goes."

"Take it," Kai insisted.

"It's not meant for cars."

"Bean, look in front of you," Kai said.

Bean looked. The other car was coming around the circular driveway. Heading straight for them.

"I'm taking it." Bean swung the wheel to the right.

The next thing Bean and Kai knew, they were airborne.

Eleven

Looking back on it, Kai wasn't sure they actually left the ground, but it sure felt like it. The front end of the hearse tilted down as if they'd just gone off the edge of a steep cliff on a sled. The path they were on veered sharply to the right. Going straight was not an option thanks to the row of golf carts parked directly in front of them. Bean spun the steering wheel to the right, and the hearse screeched and skidded, practically going up on two wheels. Kai was thrown against Bean, and in the back the surfboards banged together.

Bouncing down the path in the dark, Bean managed to straighten the hearse out. In the fringes of the headlights, Kai could see what appeared to be a low stone wall on their right and a vast open fairway on their left. Finally regaining control of the hearse, Bean started to hit the brakes.

"Don't stop," Kai said.

"Why not?"

"Keep going."

"But this isn't even a road."

"*Keep* going!"

"You're crazy," Bean said, but he did take his foot off the brake. The hearse bounced through the dark on the narrow path.

"Turn off the lights," Kai said.

Bean turned and stared at him.

"Just do it!" Kai grabbed the flashlight and rolled down the window, lighting the path in front of them with the flashlight beam. Bean killed the headlights and slowed the hearse to a crawl. The golf cart path had gone from paved to unpaved, and the hearse lumbered slowly along. Kai stuck his head out the window and looked behind them. There was no sign of following headlights.

"What do you think?" he asked Bean.

"What do I think?" Bean repeated. "You mean, *besides* the fact that you're certifiably insane?"

"What do you want to do?"

"Go home."

"I mean, right now."

"I know what you meant," Bean said. "And that's what I want to do. But somehow it doesn't appear to be an option, so I guess the next best thing is we park somewhere and lay low until those guys get tired of waiting for us."

"Okay, here," Kai said, turning off the flashlight.

Bean pulled the hearse off the path and under a large tree. He cut the engine, and everything went quiet except for loud breathing as Bean and Kai caught their breaths. It was pitch black. The leaves of the tree cut off whatever moon- and starlight would normally illuminate the car. As Kai calmed down he heard crickets chirping.

"Now what?" Bean asked in a whisper.

"We wait," Kai whispered back.

"Till when?" Bean asked.

"Till he calls again."

"How do you know he's gonna call again?"

"Bet you a quarter."

Bean didn't reply. They sat in the dark. The hearse made odd clinking noises as it cooled down, but nothing loud enough for anyone far away to hear. The crickets seemed to grow louder, as if the arrival of the strange car in the dark had only temporarily silenced them.

"How long?" Bean asked.

"Probably gonna be a while," Kai answered.

Bean sighed loudly and shook his head. "Great. And for all we know, those two creeps are out there in the dark, looking for us. I think I liked it better when you were just picking fights with Slammin' Sam and the wahoos at Screamers."

"I'm not into picking fights," said Kai.

"Yeah, you just do what you believe in your heart is right," Bean said. "Only, for some strange reason, that almost always leads to fights. Know what, Kai? I think it would be really great if you could come up with a non-violent way to do the right thing."

"I'll take it under consideration," Kai said.

They grew quiet again. It was getting late. Kai yawned.

"I cannot believe you're relaxed enough to feel tired," Bean muttered. "I keep waiting for one of those guys to jump out of the dark with an ax in his hands."

Bean's cell phone rang. Kai answered it. At first all he heard was loud music. Then Goldilocks said, "Hey, where are you guys?" Goldilocks spoke loudly over the music.

"Where are you?" Kai asked.

"Eighty-eights," Goldilocks said. "The dance place between Belle Harbor and Sun Haven. Look, screw it, you guys want those boards that bad, you can have them, okay?"

"Thanks."

Goldilocks hung up.

"Sounded like they were someplace with loud music," Bean said. "Even I could hear it."

"Yeah."

Bean sat up and reached for the key. "Guess that means we can go."

"No way."

"Why not?"

"Just wait."

"Why?"

"They're still here."

"No, they're not," said Bean. "You heard the music. They're at some bar or club somewhere."

"Sorry, partner."

Bean slumped down in the seat again.

Another fifteen minutes passed. Finally

Bean gave Kai a long sideways glance in the dark. "Come on, dude, I don't want to spend the night here."

"Okay, turn on the radio," Kai said.

"What?"

"You heard me."

Bean turned on the car radio. Kai scanned the stations until he found one he liked. He leaned close to the speaker and punched Goldilocks's phone number into the cell phone and pressed it to his ear.

"Hello?" Goldilocks answered.

"Hey, Albert, where are you?" Kai asked loudly over the music.

"Uh, Eighty-eights," Goldilocks said.

"So are we, but I don't see you," Kai said.

"*You're* at Eighty-eights?" Goldilocks asked. "How?"

"We took the back way out of the golf course," Kai said.

"What the . . . Fuck!" Goldilocks hung up.

Kai turned off the car's radio and brought down his window. Somewhere in the dark a car engine roared to life, and he heard the screech of tires. The sound grew distant as the car sped away.

Kai leaned back in his seat and smiled.

Bean stared at him in amazement. "How the . . ."

Kai felt the smile slowly leave his face. He hated to think of how he knew what Goldilocks had been up to. Mainly because he'd spent so much time around dishonest lowlifes who thought the same way Goldilocks did. It was nothing to be proud of. "We can go now."

Twelve

By the time they got back to Sun Haven, Main Street was dark and deserted. Kai was lost in thought.

"Know what I just realized?" Bean muttered. "It almost doesn't matter where we hide the boards, because all Goldilocks has to do is look for someone driving around in an old hearse. I mean, it's not like it's hard to find me."

"It's possible," Kai said.

"Why did I let you talk me into doing this?" Bean asked. "Why, why, why?"

"Because you're a good guy."

"Good and stupid," Bean grumbled. He tapped his fingers against the steering wheel.

"So where are we going to hide twelve surfboards anyway?"

"In the one place where Goldilocks won't want to look," Kai answered.

"And that would be where?"

Kai smiled at him.

"Oh, no," Bean groaned.

Next to the embalming room in the basement of the L. Balter & Son funeral home was the dressing room, where bodies were dressed in their Sunday finest and placed in whatever casket their loved ones had chosen to purchase for the occasion. On previous visits to Bean's place of residence and work, Kai had noticed that Bean and his father used a conveyor belt to send empty caskets down to the dressing room, and to bring the loaded caskets up and out to the back of the building to be placed in a hearse.

Kai stayed upstairs and fed surfboards onto the conveyor belt while Bean was downstairs in the dressing room taking them off. Once he'd finished, Kai went downstairs to help Bean store the boards safely. Ironically the caskets in the dressing room were stored on the same size sawhorses that a shaper would use for a surfboard.

"How long are we going to keep them here?" Bean asked.

"Don't know," Kai said.

"Here's an idea," said Bean. "Maybe someday I'll turn this place into the L. Balter and Son Funeral Home and Surfboard Shop. When things get slow in the undertaking business, I'll just use the embalming room as a shaping room, and I'll paint and glass the boards in here."

"You could do sponsorship deals and shape your own caskets, too," Kai said, rapping his knuckles against a heavy dark wooden casket. "Instead of making them out of wood, make them out of foam and fiberglass. And instead of painting them dark brown and black, spray paint them Day-Glo colors with cool designs."

"With sponsors' stickers," Bean quipped. "'Ladies and gentlemen, this funeral is sponsored by Volcom and Reef.' Hey, wait, forget the caskets. We could put the sponsors' stickers right on the bodies themselves for the open-casket viewing. Roberta and David Stevens bring you the body of their dearly beloved father, Morris Stevens, sponsored by Gonzo Traction Pads and Hellfire Surf Wax."

"Now *that's* sick," Kai said.

Bean twirled the end of his long braided ponytail between his fingers. "I have to say that being your friend has been a truly bizarre and unique experience." He checked his watch. "It's late and I have a feeling tomorrow's gonna be the first day in a week with any kind of rideable surf, so don't ask me to do anything else tonight, okay? You're a great guy, but I've done you all the favors I'm going to do, understood?"

"Understood," Kai said.

"Great. I'll see you tomorrow." Bean turned toward the stairs.

"Uh, Bean?" Kai said.

Bean stopped. "Now what?"

"One last favor?"

Kai's friend stiffened with anticipation. "What'd I just tell you?"

"I was just wondering if I could stay here tonight?"

Bean's shoulders sagged with relief. "Sure, Kai."

Thirteen

He and his mom were snorkeling over a shallow reef. Around them in the water half a dozen brownish-green sea turtles flapped their fins lazily and gnawed at outcroppings of coral. The turtles ranged from the size of car tires down to a large pie. Kai and his mom kept trying to touch them, but they always managed to stay just inches out of reach. It almost looked as if they were playing a game. Kai's mom finally gave up and floated to the surface to watch while Kai kept diving down and chasing the big aquatic reptiles. Just when Kai was about to give up, the largest turtle of all suddenly swam slowly past him. Kai reached out and grabbed the edge of the turtle's shell just behind the creature's head. The next thing he knew, the turtle was pulling *him through the water. The turtle stretched its head out and glanced back at him with what almost looked like a smile. . . .*

Kai opened his eyes and squinted up into the harsh yellow light of a floor lamp. He quickly covered his face with his hand. He was lying on Bean's floor and someone was talking much too loudly: "Come on, you guys. First waves in more than a week. This is no time for sleep."

In his drowsy state Kai knew the voice wasn't Bean's. He peeked through his fingers and made out the forms of Booger and Shauna standing over him.

"You get them up," he heard Shauna say. "I'll get the coffee going."

Kai's eyelids felt impossibly heavy. His whole body felt as if it was saturated with the need to sleep. He closed his eyes.

"No way, José," Booger said.

The toe of a shoe nudged him. "Go away," Kai groaned.

"You think it's fair that Shauna doesn't get to surf because you guys were out late partying last night?" Booger asked.

"Some party," Kai heard Bean mutter from his bed. But then he heard the sound of bedsprings squeaking and feet dragging on the floor. Bean had gotten up.

Kai opened his eyes again. The cruel yellow light of the floor lamp was almost painful. Through the windows, he could see that it was still dark out. "What time is it?" he asked with a yawn.

"Let's see," Booger said. "Not a minute before four thirty."

Kai groaned. He doubted he'd gotten more than three hours' sleep. That, combined with the previous night on the beach, left him feeling half dead. He managed to sit up, then closed his eyes again and let his head nod.

He was still holding on to the turtle's shell, enjoying the ride, but the water around them was turning warm and dark and smelled like coffee. . . .

"Come on, Kai," someone said.

Kai forced his eyes to open again. Booger was holding a mug of coffee under his nose. The steamy aroma warmed his face. "Thanks, dude." Kai took the mug in both hands and sipped. The coffee was hot. Somewhere in the apartment the toilet flushed and the faucet ran. The bathroom door opened, and Bean staggered out in a robe, his long black hair hanging well past his shoulders, his eyes puffy and only half open.

Kai managed to get to his feet and took his turn in the bathroom. When he came out, the pace in Bean's apartment had definitely speeded up.

"Okay, let's go!" When Booger clapped his hands it sounded like a sonic boom. "We've got waves today. Come on, let's get on them!"

Kai allowed himself to be led down the stairs and out into the cool dark predawn air. He stood half asleep while the others loaded boards and towels into the back of the hearse.

"Time to go," Booger said.

"There's only room for three in the front seat," Bean said with a yawn.

Kai imagined lying down in the back of the hearse. "I'll get in the back," he volunteered.

"No way," Booger said. "You lie down back there and we'll never get you out. You're in front. I'll get in the back."

Kai did as he was told. Shauna sat between him and Bean, who appeared to be having some difficulty getting the key into the ignition. Finally Shauna reached over and helped him get the key into the slot.

"What *were* you guys up to last night?" she asked.

"Playing Robin Hood." Bean yawned. He

turned the key, started the hearse, and pulled down the driveway beside the funeral home.

"Personally, I always think using headlights is a good idea when driving in the dark," Shauna said.

Bean groaned and flicked on the headlights.

By the time Bean pulled into the parking lot next to the boardwalk, the first dull hint of daylight had started to appear in the east. They got out of the hearse and went to the back to get their boards. It was Kai who noticed something different.

"Hey, guys," he said.

Everyone stopped what they were doing and looked at the rows of shiny new green parking meters.

"When did this happen?" Bean asked.

"Must have been last week when none of us were surfing," Shauna said.

Booger went over to one of the meters and read the fine print. "Eight A.M. to six P.M. Twenty-five cents for ten minutes."

"That's a buck and a half an hour," Bean said.

"What a pain," Booger said.

"Just another way to give surfers grief,"

Kai said. He went over and gave the meters a closer look. "See what they did? Made it an hour limit. Then you have to come back and feed in six more quarters."

"I get it," Shauna said. "It's a pain, but not that bad if you're on the beach. You just walk up and feed in the quarters and walk back. But if you're out surfing, it means coming all the way in, leaving your board on the beach, walking to the lot, feeding the meter, going back, and then paddling all the way out again."

The big yellow Hummer pulled into the lot. Lucas and Buzzy got out. Lucas was wearing surfing trunks, but Buzzy was in khaki slacks and a light blue polo shirt, so he was probably just dropping his son off. He saw Kai and his friends huddled around the meter.

"Residents will be able to go down to town hall and buy a parking permit for the summer so they won't have to feed the meters," Lucas's father announced as if he could read their minds.

"What about nonresidents?" Kai asked.

"The resorts and hotels will issue temporary parking permits based on length of stay," Buzzy replied.

"All the resorts and hotels?" Kai asked.

"Those who are members of the chamber of commerce," said Buzzy.

Curtis, of course, was the last person in the world who would ever join a chamber of commerce, so anyone staying at the Driftwood would be unable to get a temporary parking permit, and thus would be forced the feed the meter all day. By now Lucas had taken his board, crossed the boardwalk, and started down the beach. Buzzy got back into the Hummer and left.

Bean checked his watch. "Guess that means we can surf for free until eight. Then I'll have to start feeding the meter. This afternoon I'll go over to town hall and get a permit."

They picked up their boards and started toward the beach.

"You know what's amazing?" Booger said. "It's like Buzzy Frank has forgotten that he was once a kid who loved to surf. As long as Lucas can surf, he doesn't give a crap what happens to anyone else."

"Survival of the fittest," Bean said.

They crossed the boardwalk and headed down the beach. The waves were waist high, coming in sets.

"Oh, man." Bean grunted in appreciation. "Am I glad to see this."

"The intervals seem a little longer than usual," Booger said, referring to the time between the waves.

"So it gives you a little more time to get into position to catch a wave?" Shauna guessed.

"You got it," said Kai.

"Primo conditions," Bean said as he kneeled down and started to wax his board. "Thank you, Kahuna, for giving us this day."

Kai also started to wax, but out of the corner of his eye he noticed something strange. Lucas had not gone into the water. Instead he was standing at the tidemark and staring down at the sand.

"What's he doing?" Booger asked in a low voice.

Kai looked more closely and saw that the sand near the water was dotted with jellyfish. Most were either clear shapeless blobs, or clear and flat like a see-through pancake. But here and there were larger ugly jellyfish with reddish brown centers and short tendrils. Now Kai knew why Lucas had not gone into the water.

Bean continued to wax his board.

"Uh, Bean?" Kai said.

"Don't sweat it," Bean said as if he knew what Kai was going to say. "I know it's kind of disgusting, but the clear ones won't hurt you."

"What about the big ugly red-brown ones?" Booger asked.

"Try to stay away from 'em," Bean said.

"That's easy for you to say," Booger said. "You're on a board most of the time. But I'm in the water."

"Sorry, Boogs." Bean strapped on his leash and headed for the water. "But neither rain, nor snow nor gloom of night shall stay this noble courier from the swift completion of his appointed rounds."

"What's he babbling about?" Booger asked.

"I think it's like the post office motto, or something," said Shauna.

"He's postal, all right," said Booger.

Meanwhile Kai finished waxing and, trying not to think about the jellyfish, followed Bean into the surf. It felt great to be back in the water again, and the first few paddles were okay, but then Kai felt something gelatinous brush against his fingertips. He automatically jerked his arm out of the water. Looking down he saw four or five small clear jellyfish, barely visible below the surface. It was gross, but so far Bean was right. Unlike the small blue-and-purple man-of-wars that sometimes appeared around Kauai, and could deliver a searingly painful sting, these jellyfish seemed harmless.

Kai continued to paddle, occasionally feeling that eerie gelatinous sensation of a jellyfish brush against his fingertips or palm. Finally he got outside where Bean was sitting on his long board, waiting for a wave. Straddling his short board, Kai was in the water up to his rib cage. Jellyfish floated around him, and now and then he felt one slide past his legs.

"I guess you've surfed in these things before," he said to Bean.

"Every August, dude. Look, they're not so bad." Bean dipped his hand into the water and actually picked up a clear, pancake-shaped one. "These guys are pretty cool. Watch." Bean pulled his arm back and whipped it forward, throwing the flat round jellyfish like a Frisbee.

"I'm not sure whether that's cool or completely sick," Kai said.

Booger joined them. On his bodyboard only his shoulders and head were out of the water. The rest of him was submerged, and liable to come into contact with jellyfish at any moment. "This . . . is . . . so . . . freaking . . . gross," he groaned. "I swear, if it wasn't for the fact there've been no waves for the past week, I would be out of this freaking water so fast."

Shauna was the next to arrive. Once she got outside, she lay flat on her board with her arms and feet completely out of the water. "I can't believe I'm out here. There must be something seriously wrong with me."

"It's called stoke," Bean said.

"'Psycho' is a better word," Shauna said.

Bean scooped up a small round clear one in his palm. "I told you guys, these things are harmless."

"So's toilet water, but I wouldn't go swimming in it," Booger shot back.

Lucas was still on the shore, his hands on his hips, staring down at the beach as if he couldn't meet their eyes.

"You can bet that if Buzzy was around, Lucas would be out here right now," Booger said, and then lowered his voice and imitated Lucas's father. "You want to win, son, you've got to learn to rip in every condition. Ankle-slappers, jellyfish, red tide, monsoon, raw sewage, hurricane, icebergs, sea snakes . . . You think any of those things ever stopped Kelly Slater? Hell, no. Why, I remember one time in the Sahara Desert, we didn't even have water. You think that stopped us from surfing? Damn right it didn't."

Kai and the others chuckled. As if Lucas somehow knew what they were thinking, he flung himself onto his board and began to paddle out. At the same time, a new set started to come in. With the extra-long intervals, Kai, Bean, and the others all managed to catch waves for their first rides in a week.

"That was so great!" Shauna cried as she started to paddle back out.

"I take back every bad thing I ever said about jellyfish," Booger chimed in as he paddled out beside her.

When they got back outside, Lucas was there, bobbing on his board. Kai and the others nodded at him but didn't say a word. While they waited for the next set, Kai noticed that Lucas spent more time scanning the water around him for jellyfish than watching for waves. Another set came in. Bean paddled for a wave but missed it. Shauna tried to catch one, but was too deep under the peak and pearled. Kai caught one and had a nice ride down the line. When he kicked out and started to paddle back, he discovered Booger kicking out beside him.

"Good ride, huh?" Booger said.

"Yeah. You got the wave after mine?" Kai asked.

"Right. You see Lucas?"

"What about him?" Kai asked.

"He had at least two easy shots and let both pass," Booger said. "I think it's because he's afraid to bite it in the sea of jellyfish."

"Can't say I totally blame him," Kai said, now and then feeling that weird gelatinous sensation against his finger tips as he paddled. It was almost like swimming through liquid Jell-O.

Back on the beach, Derek, Everett, and Sam showed up. All three stopped at the tide mark and studied the jellyfish that lay dying and drying in the sun. Kai was impressed with Everett's ability to move back and forth between Lucas's crew and Kai and his friends. The kid clearly had a mind of his own.

After a few moments Derek and Everett got into the water and started to paddle out. But Sam stayed on the shore. Another set came in and Bean caught a wave. Once again Shauna went for one and pearled. Kai paddled over to her while she climbed back onto her board.

"I hate to say this, but you might be better off back at Sewers," Kai said, knowing that the waves there were slower and easier to catch.

"But these are better rides," Shauna said as she started to paddle back out.

"And harder to catch," Kai said.

Shauna shrugged. "Gotta learn sometime."

She and Kai made it outside. By now Derek and Everett were out there.

"Welcome to Jellyfish City," Kai said.

"As long as they don't sting, I don't care," Everett said.

On the shore Sam turned and started back up the beach with his board under his arm. With Lucas and Derek within earshot, Kai and the others chose not to comment, but it definitely looked like the tough guy had been scared off.

Kai sat on his board, watching for the next set, but he could see nothing promising on the horizon. Out of nowhere he heard a splash near him. He looked at the widening ripples in the water and saw one of the flat, pancake-shaped jellyfish bob to the surface. A moment later there was another splash and another round, flat jellyfish appeared. Kai looked up. Either seagulls were dropping them out of the sky, or . . .

Splat! Something hit him in the back of the head. Kai spun around. Bean and Booger were both looking off into the distance as if gazing at some faraway sight, but both had smiles on their faces. Kai reached into the water and picked up one of the flat, round jellyfish. He was surprised by how thick and tough it felt in his hand. Much sturdier than he'd imagined a jellyfish would feel. He wound up and threw the jellyfish at Bean. He missed and was reaching into the water to find another one when both Bean and Booger turned and fired jellyfish back at him. Obviously they'd been waiting for Kai to retaliate.

It was a full-scale jellyfish war. Everett joined in, and so did Derek. Jellyfish, and pieces of jellyfish, were flying everywhere. The jellyfish were difficult to aim and tended to break apart in the air, so the only way to ensure a direct hit was to move closer to the intended target. Soon Bean, Booger, Kai, Everett, and Derek were all within twenty feet of one another, throwing as hard as they could. The broken jellyfish left a thin layer of slime on their hands and smelled fishy, but this was war, and war was not pretty.

Shauna and Lucas paddled out of range and watched. The battle continued until every jellyfish within reach and been reduced to tiny unthrowable morsels. The warriors were left bobbing on their boards, breathing hard, and grinning. Kai brought his slimy hands to his nose and sniffed. The fishy smell was stronger than he'd expected. "Gross!"

Bean rolled off his board and dove, then reappeared on the surface with a handful of sand he'd scooped off the bottom. He rubbed the sand between his hands to get the slime off. Kai and the others dove down and did the same. The sand got most of the slime off, but the smell remained.

Lucas paddled back toward them. "You guys are completely sick," he said.

Kai and the others grinned. Kai couldn't help noticing that, for the first time, his friends and Lucas and his crew were mixed together into one group.

"Hey, if God didn't want us to throw jelly-fish, he wouldn't have made them so easy to pick up," Everett said.

"It's not like they're good for anything else," added Booger.

"What? You never had a jellyfish omelet?" asked Bean.

The others groaned.

"That's awful," Shauna said.

"Beyond fricken gross," said Lucas.

"Don't knock it till you've tried it," Bean said. "I like mine mixed with cheddar cheese and bacon."

Everyone told Bean to shut up. It was Kai who noticed that Bean had stopped smiling and was staring toward the shore. He turned and looked. Goldilocks was standing on the beach.

"Oh, crap," Bean muttered. "Now we're really toast."

Fourteen

Goldilocks stood on the beach, glaring at them. He was holding some kind of club in one hand and tapping it against his palm.

"What do we do?" Bean asked Kai.

Kai checked his watch. It was a little after seven A.M. "Ask him what he's doing up at this hour. I would have thought this was kind of early for him."

"I'm serious," Bean said.

"Who's that?" Shauna asked.

"No one important," Kai said.

Shauna frowned as if she knew that wasn't true.

"Why's he got that club?" Booger asked.

"Guess he likes it," Kai said.

"You know what he's going to do, don't you?" Bean said. "He's going to stay there until we get tired of surfing and go in. He knows we can't stay out here all day."

"That's okay with me," Kai said.

"Dude, get serious," Bean said. "You know he's a badass and you know what he wants. He didn't come here just to watch us surf."

Derek paddled close to them. "You know that guy?"

It took Kai a second to realize that this was the first time he'd ever heard Derek speak.

"Not really, but we've had some, er, business dealings with him," Kai answered.

Derek dipped one eyebrow and smiled slightly, as if regarding Kai in a new light. "Business, huh?"

"This is crazy," Bean said anxiously. "I can't enjoy surfing with him standing there like that."

"You got a problem with him?" Derek asked.

"No. Yeah. I don't know," Bean answered. "It should be Kai's problem, but somehow Kai has a way of making all of his problems my problems too. Of course, he isn't worried about it. Meanwhile, I'm totally freaked."

"Okay, Bean." Kai started to reach down to take off his leash.

"What are you doing?" Bean asked.

"I'll take care of it," Kai said, sliding off his board. "Then you won't have to worry."

"You're going in . . . *alone?*" Bean asked in total disbelief.

"He may be a badass, but he's not going to kill me on the beach in front of witnesses," Kai said, and handed Bean the ankle strap connected to his leash.

"Why aren't you taking your board?" Shauna asked.

"Can't risk getting it damaged," Kai said.

"I'm going with you," said Derek, sliding off his board and pushing it toward Everett.

"Why you?" Bean asked.

"I never liked that guy," Derek said.

"You know him?" Bean asked.

"Oh, yeah," Derek said. "We've done business too."

Derek and Kai started to swim in.

"Hold up, guys," said Everett. "I'll go with you."

He slipped off his board and gave his and Derek's leashes to Booger to hold.

Kai, Derek, and Everett swam toward shore,

got to the shallows, and stepped out of the waves. Goldilocks stood on the dry side of the tide mark tapping the club ominously against his palm. With seawater dripping down his face, Kai stopped a dozen feet away and stood on the wet sand. Derek and Everett stopped with him.

"Reinforcements, huh?" Goldilocks smirked and tapped the club in his hand.

"What do you want?" Kai asked.

"You know what I want."

"They're not yours," Kai said.

"I paid for 'em," Goldilocks said. "They're mine."

"No way," Kai said. "They weren't Big Dave's and he had no right to sell them to you."

Goldilocks twitched. There was no doubt in Kai's mind now that it was Big Dave who'd sold him Curtis's boards.

"Then I want my money back," Goldilocks said.

"Can't help you there, either," Kai said. "That's between you and Big Dave."

Goldilocks narrowed his eyes. "You got this all figured out, don't you?"

"Hey, you play with fire, you get burned,"

Kai said. "Even a four-year-old knows that."

Goldilocks charged. Kai quickly reached down to the sand and grabbed one of the dozens of jellyfish that had washed up on the beach. He threw it, and it hit Goldilocks in the chest but didn't stop him. Kai doubted Goldilocks even felt it. He also doubted he had time to grab another jellyfish before Goldilocks nailed him with the club. He was turning to dive for the water when he heard a loud *splat!*

Kai looked back. Goldilocks had stopped. He was standing still with a totally disgusted expression on his face as he wiped clear jellyfish gook off his jaw.

Splat! A jellyfish hit him in the forehead.

Kai looked to his right, where Derek was picking up another jellyfish. He wound up and hurled it like a baseball pitcher. Unfortunately Goldilocks ducked out of the way of that one.

Splat! Goldilocks was so busy ducking Derek's throw that he didn't see the one Everett threw. It hit him in the ear. By now Kai had time to pick up another jellyfish and throw it, too.

Splat!

Splat!

Splat!

No matter which way Goldilocks turned, Kai, Everett, or Derek nailed him. In no time the guy was covered with clear jellyfish gook. Goldilocks started to curse up a storm, swearing and threatening that he'd kill them, but Kai and his friends just kept pelting him. Finally the guy put his hands over his head and face and turned away, jogging up the beach until he was out of flying jellyfish range.

He stopped and glared at them. "This ain't over, dipshits."

"Oh, no?" Derek said. "Then come on back."

Goldilocks stormed toward the parking lot, still wiping jellyfish off his face.

Kai exchanged high fives with Derek and Everett.

"Way to go, guys," Kai said. "And seriously, thanks."

"Anytime," Derek said. "That was fun."

"I'm lucky you guys had good aim," Kai said. "He almost got me."

"Not a chance." Derek pointed at a dead horseshoe crab lying on its back in the sun, with flies buzzing around it. "If he'd gotten any closer, I was going to nail him in the face with that."

Kai looked down at the dead horseshoe. Dead jellyfish may have been gross, but dead horseshoe crabs were beyond gross. And yet he had no doubt that Derek would have picked it up and smashed Goldilocks with it.

By now Bean, Booger, and Lucas had come in to shore. Bean had Kai's board with him. Shauna was still out at Screamers with Everett's and Derek's boards. "Dudes, that was crazy! 'Attacker Repelled by Jellyfish Defense!'" Bean said, like he was quoting a newspaper headline.

Everett and Derek squatted down and scrubbed their hands vigorously with wet sand to try to get the jellyfish slime off. Then they both dove into the surf and swam back out to the break, where Shauna was waiting with their boards.

"Anyone else going back out?" Booger asked.

"I hate to say this," Bean said. "Even though this is the first time in a week that we've got waves, I think I'm gonna split. Something about seeing that guy here has kind of killed it for me for today."

"I know what you're saying," Kai said.

"I'm thinking of packing it in and heading over to Teddy's. I'm in the middle of a couple of projects."

"Okay, guys, catch you later," Booger said, and picked up his bodyboard.

That reminded Kai of something. "Can you do me a favor, Booger? When you get out there, tell Shauna to try to set up a little farther from the curl, okay? Like out on the shoulder of the wave. I think she's starting too deep under the peak. And tell her not to forget to angle the board."

"Sure thing, dude." Booger headed back out.

That left Lucas, Bean, and Kai on the beach. Kai and Bean were about to pick up their boards and go when Lucas said, "Wait a minute."

Kai straightened up. "Yeah?"

"Did I hear you say something to that guy about Big Dave?" Lucas asked.

Kai and Bean shared a look. Neither answered. But in a way, their silence was an answer.

"So what's going on?" Lucas asked. "I mean, what was that about?"

"He had a bunch of boards that belong to Curtis," Kai said. "So Bean and I took them back."

"And what's that got to do with Big Dave?" Lucas asked.

"Maybe you should ask your father," Kai said.

Lucas frowned, but didn't say anything more. He picked up his board and headed for the water. Bean and Kai walked up the beach with their boards under their arms.

"How come you didn't tell him about Big Dave?" Bean asked.

"Gotta have proof," Kai said. "I mean, you and I both know that he was almost definitely involved, but why should anyone else believe us?"

"How're you gonna get proof?" Bean asked. "Nobody saw him sell the boards to Goldilocks, and you know for sure neither of them would ever admit it."

"You never know," Kai said. "Stranger things have happened."

Bean stared at him. "You are a mysterious dude, Kai. But I'm past the point where I'd ever think of betting against you."

They reached the parking lot and headed for the hearse. Suddenly Bean stopped and muttered, "Shit."

Fifteen

All four tires on the hearse had been slashed and were completely flat.

"Crap, crap, crap," Bean growled as he and Kai walked around the car, inspecting the damage.

Kai felt awful. "It's my fault, dude. If I hadn't gotten you involved in this, it never would have happened."

Bean didn't argue. He unlocked the car door and got out his cell phone. "Good thing I've got Triple-A. They'll tow it to the nearest station for free."

"Bet they don't replace the tires for free," Kai said.

Bean shook his head.

Kai waited with Bean until the flatbed truck came. They couldn't use a tow truck to tow a car with four flat tires. Kai had no idea what car tires cost, only that they couldn't be cheap because nothing on a car was cheap. He and Bean watched as the driver winched the hearse onto the back of the truck.

"Know what's weird?" Bean said. "I'm pissed, but I'm not sorry. I know we did the right thing."

"I'll make it up to you," Kai said.

"Thanks, dude, I appreciate the thought. Catch you later."

Bean got into the truck with the driver. Kai watched them pull out of the parking lot, then he walked over to Teddy's. Behind her workshop he rinsed himself off with a garden hose, then stood in the sunlight and let the rays dry him. He let himself into the workshop. The lights were off. "Teddy?"

No one answered. That was unusual. Teddy was almost always in the shop by that time of the morning.

Kai crossed the yard to Teddy's house, stepped up on the porch, and rang the bell. He waited, listening to the wind chimes clink. No one answered, but Kai had a feeling she was home. Of course, she didn't have to answer her door if she didn't want to, but it made Kai uncomfortable. Teddy lived alone, and there was always a chance, no matter how slim, that she'd fallen and hurt herself or otherwise needed help for some reason.

He stepped off the porch and walked around the house, peeking in the windows. He found Teddy in her kitchen, sitting at the table with a cup and a cigarette.

"Hey," he said through the window.

Teddy looked up. While there were no tears visible, her glassy eyes were puffy and red rimmed. That could have been either from lack of sleep or crying. Maybe it didn't matter.

"Go away," she said.

"I didn't know you smoked," Kai said.

"I don't." Her words hung in the air like the smoke drifting up from the embers of the cigarette.

"How come you're not in the shop?"

"I said, go away."

"Come on, Teddy."

She took a drag on the cigarette, then exhaled a cloud. "Fucking Buzzy did it. He cut me off."

"He got a new shaper?"

"A guy over in Fairport."

"Any good?"

Teddy made a face. "Do you really think Buzzy cares? As long as he makes his money he could give a crap."

"Maybe you could work for one of the other shops," Kai said. "Like Fairport Surf."

Teddy smirked. "Rick Petersen would be lucky to sell one custom board a month."

"What about opening your own place?" Kai asked.

Teddy's eyebrows dipped for a moment. "Oh, right, you and me as partners against Buzzy Frank. How could I forget?"

"We don't have to be partners."

"That's for damn sure."

"Come on, Teddy." Kai braced himself for some sharp rebuke, so he was surprised when she turned away from him. He heard her sniff and saw her shoulders tremble.

In a cracking voice she said, "For the love of God, Kai, go away!"

Kai went back across the lawn to the workshop, let himself inside, and flicked on the lights. He turned on the radio and got to work buffing a board. Propped in the corner of the room was a nine-footer—shaped, but not yet glassed.

It was a "spec" board. One Teddy worked on in her spare time in the hope of selling.

Kai had an idea. What if he took the round *T-L* logo he'd done for T-licious and turned it into a *TL* logo that stood for Theodora Lombard. He could copy the style of the *TL* Teddy always placed on the stringer of each board. Maybe, if she actually saw what her own brand of custom board would look like, it might inspire her to start her own business. Kai glanced out the window toward the house. It would take a while to draw the logo. There was no way of telling if, or when, Teddy might decide to get to work that day.

Then again, maybe it didn't matter.

Teddy had an airbrush, some spray cans of acrylic lacquer, brushes, tape, pencils, and enough acrylic paints for Kai to do what he needed to do. It was basically the same circular design with *T* and *L* in the center. Instead of "Team T-licious" in fancy script forming the perimeter, it would now say "Theodora Lombard Custom Boards."

Kai wanted it to be perfect, and it took almost the entire day just to get the outline and lettering right. He was about to start coloring when the workshop door opened and Teddy stepped in. Her eyes focused on the spec board and she scowled. She stepped closer. Kai instinctively moved back, not just to give her room, but in case she decided to grab the power planer and bash him in the skull with it.

"What do you think you're doing?" she asked, still staring at the board.

"I thought maybe if you saw what it would look like . . ." Kai's words trailed off as he realized how stupid that must have sounded.

"What it would look like?" Teddy repeated. "There is no *it* for it to look like. There's no Theodora Lombard custom surfboard company, except in *your* imagination. All you've done is ruin a perfectly good board. And that means you now owe me for two boards, not just one."

Kai picked up a sheet of sandpaper. "I can sand it off."

"No, you can't," Teddy said. "Not today. I've seen enough of you for one day."

Sixteen

Dinner on Pete's Hubba Hubba terrace had become a regular event. Not everyone showed up every night—and sometimes Kai and his friends still had pizza at Spazzy's—but if you were going anywhere else, Pete's was the place. Lucas and his brahs had their regular table; Kai and his friends had theirs. Everett was still the only one among them who felt comfortable at both.

The rest of the crowd was mostly vacationers. Pete's specialized in catering to teenage tourist kids who didn't want to be seen eating lunch or dinner with their parents. These kids were easy to spot—their skin was either pale because they'd just started vacation, or bright red from too much sun too fast. It was only in contrast to them that Kai realized how darkly tan he and his friends had become since May.

Pete's was set up like a school cafeteria. You stood on line and got a tray. Only, instead of picking the food from inside a glass counter, you placed an order, then slid the tray down the rail and picked up drinks. By the time you got to the other end where the cashier was, your chili cheesesteak or slice of pizza or whatever was ready to be picked up.

When Kai got on line he noticed that Shauna was ahead of him. He was about to say hello (and see if he could jump the line to join her) when he realized that she was standing next to Derek, and that they were talking. Not only talking, but smiling as well. Kai decided to keep his place in line and not bother them.

A few moments later he picked up his Hubba juice and chili cheeseburger and headed out to the terrace. He saw Shauna sitting by herself at their regular table. Derek had gone over to Lucas's table to sit with the brahs.

"Hey," Kai said, joining Shauna.

"Hi, Kai." Shauna flashed him a smile.

"So'd you finally manage to catch a wave at Screamers today?" he asked.

"Oh, yes!" Shauna lit up excitedly. "I had this one ride. It was incredible! Probably on the biggest wave I ever rode . . . I know that's not saying much for me, but still it was so awesome! I was sideways and everything! Like I could almost reach out and touch the face. I wish you could have seen it!"

Kai smiled. Hearing her talk about that ride was the definition of pure stoke. But then her expression changed and became more somber. "I heard about Bean's car. Why'd that guy slash his tires?"

"He got involved in something that he should have stayed away from," was all Kai cared to say.

"Bean did?"

"No, the other guy," Kai said. "Although, I guess right now Bean feels that way too."

"Do you think the other guy'll come back again?"

"Don't know," Kai said. "If he does, we'll just have to deal with him."

They ate quietly for a few moments. Kai noticed that Shauna glanced over at Lucas's table where Derek was sitting. It was hard to imagine those two having anything to talk about, and Kai wasn't sure how he felt about it.

"Hey, guys." Spazzy joined them, placing a slice and a Coke on the table. "How was it this morning?"

"Not bad if you don't mind the occasional mouthful of jellyfish," Shauna said.

"I thought you would've been out there," said Kai.

"Believe me, I would've, but big sister put her foot down," Spazzy said. "As far as she's concerned, her brother and jellyfish do not swim in the same ocean."

"Even though most of them are harmless?" Shauna asked.

"Most, but not all," Spazzy said. "Don't forget who you're dealing with. Jillian read about them in the newspaper yesterday and it was straight to the Internet to find out what kind they were and which might be harmful. So it turns out that the big ones with reddish centers are called Lion's Manes, and they have tentacles that can cause burning and skin irritations. That was all she had to read and there was no way I was surfing."

"Sorry, dude," Kai said.

"Hey," Spazzy said, "she's come a long way. At least she lets me surf when there are no jellyfish."

"Maybe it's a good thing you weren't here," Shauna said. "Would you believe these guys had a jellyfish fight?"

"No way." Spazzy grinned.

"Not with the Lion's Mane ones," Kai explained. "Just the round, flat clear ones."

"Those are called moon jellies," Spazzy told them, shaking his head wearily. "Ask me anything you want to know about jellyfish. My sister made me learn every single type found in the northern Atlantic, so I could identify the dangerous ones. I mean, she *tested* me."

"She cares about you," Shauna said, and checked her watch. "Dinner break's over. Back to work. See you guys later."

Kai watched her get up. As she left she glanced at the table where Derek was sitting, caught his eye and gave him a little wave.

The sun was setting and a slight breeze swept across the terrace. Unlike the breezes of a summer evening, which often blew warm and moist, this one had a dryness and chill to it. Kai recognized what it meant.

Spazzy twitched and blinked rapidly, licked

the back of his hand and sniffed it, then made some squeaking sounds. Kai knew him well enough by now to know that when he got going like that, it meant something was on his mind.

"Summer's ending," he said.

Funny how they were both thinking the same thing.

"I'm gonna have to go back to school." Spazzy didn't sound happy.

"I thought you liked it," Kai said.

"It's okay. It's just . . . You know, it's full of kids like me. I mean, they don't all have Tourette's syndrome, but they all have something that makes them look and act different. And no matter how many times they tell us that our handicaps don't really matter, and we're just as good as everyone else, and that it's not really our fault and blah, blah, blah, you never really forget that you're different. You never really believe that there's nothing wrong, or bad. You never stop wondering why this had to happen to you and what did you do to deserve it. Until this past month I never really believed that it would ever be different from that, you know? That's why my whole world used to be my sister and a few friends at school and maybe a couple of people like Ms. Lantz."

Kai scowled. He couldn't remember who she was.

"My teacher out in California," Spazzy said. "The one who taught me to surf."

"Right."

"And that's why this last month has been so amazing," Spazzy went on. "For the first time in my life I really did feel like it was okay to have Tourette's syndrome. Or at least, I was finally with a bunch of friends who honestly didn't care and weren't just pretending it didn't matter if I acted weird. It's hard to leave that, you know?"

Kai nodded, but he was distracted by Lucas, Derek, and Sam, who'd finished eating and were coming toward their table.

"Hey," Lucas said.

"Hey." Kai nodded back. His eye caught Derek's. "Thanks again for helping me out this morning."

"No sweat," Derek said. "It was kind of fun."

"That's some arm you've got," Kai said.

"I used to play center field for my high school team," Derek said. "My favorite thing was nailing guys trying to score on sacrifice flies."

"So my dad wants me to give you a message," Lucas said. "He says he'll pay the entry fee for you to compete in the Northeast Championship."

Kai felt his eyebrows dip with puzzlement.

"He thinks I need someone to push me," Lucas said. "Otherwise I'll be too complacent."

"What the hell's that mean?" Sam asked.

"Means he'll think he's already good enough to win, so he won't work that hard," Kai said. "Then he'll get into the competition and find himself losing to guys he didn't know would be there."

"It's like having a sparring partner," Derek said.

"How come your dad doesn't want me to do that?" Sam asked Lucas. "And he can pay for my entry fee too."

Nobody answered.

"So what do you say?" Lucas asked Kai.

"I don't know," Kai said.

"You never know," Sam said. "That's what you always say."

Lucas turned on him angrily. "Will you shut up?"

"What did I say?" Sam looked surprised.

"He's the guy who had the highest single-wave score at Fairport, remember?" Lucas said of Kai. "That's why my father picked him and not you."

Sam shrank back.

"Tell you what," Kai said. "I'll be your sparring partner until the competition. Maybe I'll enter; maybe I won't. But you won't know. And anyway, there'll be way better surfers there than me, so it'll be good for you."

"Deal." Lucas held out his hand. Kai shook it. "Tomorrow morning. Sunrise?"

"See you then," Kai said.

Lucas and his brahs headed off, leaving Kai and Spazzy at their table.

"If Buzzy's willing to pay, you should enter," Spazzy said.

"I wish it was that simple," Kai said.

"What's the problem?"

"It's a long story. I promise I'll tell you some time, but you know what it's like when everybody keeps asking you the same thing over and over?"

"Are you kidding?" Spazzy replied. "You know how many times I've been asked what's wrong with me? Believe me, I know how it feels."

"Thanks, dude."

The breeze blew, and the bolder sparrows hopped around at Kai's feet, pecking at crumbs.

"I'm thinking of entering," Spazzy suddenly said.

The announcement caught Kai by surprise.

"I figure I might go a couple of heats before getting knocked out," Spazzy said. "After all, I made it to the finals at Fairport, didn't I?"

Kai nodded. But he knew the reason Spazzy had made it to the finals at Fairport had been partly luck and partly because Kai had gotten himself disqualified on purpose.

"I mean, think about it," Spazzy went on. "The Northeast Championships are gonna be covered by all the magazines and Web sites. Those media guys are always looking for something new and different to write about. So here's this kid with Tourette's syndrome actually competing in a major surfing event. If that gets covered, it's gonna do a lot for how people look at kids with Tourette's."

"I agree," Kai said. "Just don't forget that this is going to be a big-time event. It's gonna make Fairport look like a kickball game. All of us could get blown out in the first heat."

"Hey, don't I know it," Spazzy said. "So that's why I wanted to ask you if maybe tomorrow morning I could come out there too."

Kai smiled. "You don't have to ask. Remember, as far as I'm concerned, Screamers is open to everyone. Only, what about your sister and the jellyfish?"

Spazzy grinned. "Leave it to me, dude."

Seventeen

Later Kai walked into the office of the Driftwood Motel. Two guys were standing at the counter, ringing the bell. Kai recognized them immediately. One was thin, with tousled blond hair. He had tattoos on both arms and looked like he was in his twenties. The other was stocky, with dark hair shaved close to his head and black tattoos on both shoulders. Kai had spoken to them the first time he set foot in the backyard at the Driftwood.

"You know where Curtis is?" the stocky one asked. "We've been ringing the bell for fifteen minutes."

The thin blond guy narrowed his eyes. "Hey, haven't I seen you before?"

"Yeah, about three months ago," Kai said. "In the back."

The blond guy nodded. "Right. You're the one who said we could probably get tubed down at Screamers." He nudged his buddy with his elbow. "You remember, don't you?"

"Yeah." The stocky guy grinned. "So you been tubed at Screamers yet?"

"A couple of times," Kai said. "The swell out of the southeast has to be just right, you know?"

Both guys frowned. "No, we wouldn't know," said the stocky one.

"And I think you're full of shit," said the skinny one. He turned and rang the bell again. "Where the hell is Curtis?"

"I'll see if he's here." Kai went around the counter and knocked on the door behind it. "Hey, Curtis," he called. "You got some visitors."

No answer.

"Guess he's not there," said the stocky one.

Kai pressed a finger to his lips and moved his ear close to the door. Inside he heard glass clink. He knocked on the door again. "Come on, old man, you've got some paying customers."

"Fuck 'em," Curtis muttered from inside.

Kai turned away from the door and pulled open a drawer behind the counter. Inside lay a jumble of mixed-up keys. Kai looked up at the guys. "What room do you usually stay in?"

"Twenty-three," said the blond one.

Kai sorted through the keys and found #23. "That'll be forty-five bucks."

"We pay when we check out," said the dark-haired one.

"Not this time," said Kai.

The two guys shared a look. The blond one shrugged. "Go ahead, pay him."

The dark-haired guy peeled off two twenties and a five. Kai handed over the key. "You guys don't mind jellyfish, do you?"

"Clear ones or bluish with tendrils?" asked the blond guy.

"Mostly clear," said Kai.

"Pain in the ass, but that's life," the blond guy said.

"Good, see you at Screamers tomorrow," Kai said.

The dark-haired guy made a face. "That break's owned by the locals."

"Not anymore," said Kai. "And definitely not when the jellyfish are around."

The thin blond guy with the tousled hair gave Kai a curious look, as if maybe he wasn't so full of shit after all. "Okay, thanks."

Both guys went back out. Kai tried the door to Curtis's apartment. It opened, but the room inside was dark. No surf videos on the TV. Kai stood in the doorway and waited for his eyes to adjust. The room smelled faintly of body odor and rotting garbage. Kai had the feeling Curtis had been in here for days. He could barely make out the form of Curtis sitting on the couch.

"Kind of dark in here, isn't it?" Kai asked.

"Metaphor for my life," Curtis answered.

"Is that what they mean by self-pity?" Kai asked.

"Fuck off and leave me alone."

"I've got some money for you," Kai said. "It's not much, but I'd guess every little bit helps."

Curtis didn't reply.

"Come on, old man."

"I've hit rock bottom, grom. There ain't no where to go. The Feds are gonna make me sell this place for back taxes. Imagine getting to this point in your life and you don't have squat."

"What about the tax attorney?" Kai asked.

"He helped, but this place is going just the same."

"But you always knew you'd give it up someday, didn't you?" Kai asked.

"Sure I did," Curtis said. "Just like I know I'll die someday. Only that don't make it any easier when the time comes."

"Well, you may not have this place much longer, but I can show you something you didn't know you had," Kai said.

"What's that?"

"You have to come see for yourself."

Curtis didn't budge. "What the hell are you talking about?"

"I'm talking about showing you something you'll be glad to see."

"A treasure chest filled with gold?"

"Not quite."

"Then I ain't interested."

"Believe me, old man, you will be."

"Don't play games with me, grom. The fuse is short and the powder exceedingly dry."

"Trust me."

"Trust you? What's that supposed to mean?"

"Why don't you give it a chance and come see?"

It wasn't easy, but Kai finally got Curtis off the couch and through the door. When they stepped outside into the low, orange, predusk sunlight, the older man stopped and shielded his eyes with his hands. "Lord, it's bright out here."

"The sun's going to be down in twenty minutes," Kai said.

"It always this bright this late?" Curtis asked.

"Only when you haven't left your apartment for two days," Kai said.

"We goin' far?"

"Couple of blocks."

Curtis took a step and almost stumbled off the walk. Kai grabbed his arm and steadied him.

"Maybe we ought to take a cab," Curtis muttered.

"The walk'll do you good."

"A shot of JD would do me better."

"I think you've had enough of those for now," Kai said.

But Curtis shook his arm free. "What are you, my nursemaid?" He started off with a determined limp. Kai stood still behind him. "Uh, Curtis?"

The older man stopped and spun around. "What now?"

"Wrong direction." Kai pointed in the other direction.

"Well, you should have said so." With equal determination Curtis started back. They walked though town and stopped outside L. Balter & Son.

"We're here," Kai said.

Curtis looked up at the funeral home. "Has my time come, oh angel of death?"

"Not quite."

"You sure you're not the grim reaper disguised as a grom?"

"Pretty sure," Kai said. "Let's go around to the back."

"Whoa." Curtis didn't move. "We ain't really goin' in there are we?"

"We are if you want to see what I've got for you."

"Let me guess, a new body to replace this piece of junk?"

"Sorry."

"Darn." Curtis started to walk, then stopped. "Wait a minute. You ain't gonna perform one of those operations where they drain out all your blood and replace it with other stuff like they did to Keith Richards, are ya?"

"Who's Keith Richards?" Kai asked.

"Christ," Curtis grumbled. "Make me feel old, why don'tcha?"

They went around to the back. Kai noticed that the hearse had all new shiny black tires. He rang the bell. Footsteps came down the stairs and Bean opened the door.

"Hey, Kai," he said. It wasn't the warmest greeting Kai had ever received, but he couldn't blame Bean for being a little ticked off.

"This where you live?" Curtis winced, obviously grossed out by the idea that Bean lived with dead people.

"Look at it this way," Bean said. "My roommates are really quiet and they never steal any of my stuff out of the refrigerator."

"That is sick," Kai said.

But Curtis grinned. "I like it."

"We're here so Curtis can see what we've got for him," Kai said, winking quickly at Bean to warn him not to give away their secret.

"Oh, yeah," Bean said. "I can see why he might be interested."

"So, is this a good time?" Kai asked.

"Well, the body's not quite ready," Bean said.

"What the hell?" Curtis blurted out. "Body? I don't want to see no damn body."

"You sure?" Kai asked him.

Curtis hesitated. "Well, not unless it's Buzzy Frank's. But the last I heard he was alive and well and counting his money."

"I guess now's as good a time as any," Bean said, and held open the door for them to go in.

Kai went in, but Curtis didn't move. "Somethin' about this don't feel right."

"Hey, old man, you really think I'd do anything bad to you?" Kai asked.

Curtis let out a major sigh and went in. Bean led them downstairs. At the bottom of the stairs he turned on the hall light. To the right was the embalming room. To the left was the dressing room.

Bean was just about to lead them into the dressing room when Kai caught sight of what was on the embalming table and got an idea.

"Aren't we going this way?" Kai gestured toward the embalming room.

"What?" Bean scowled.

Kai made a face indicating that Bean should just go along and not ask questions. Bean rolled his eyes as if to say, *"Okay, but I'm getting tired of going along with these crazy ideas of yours."*

Lying on his back on the embalming table was the corpse of a large man with a big belly, heavy limbs, and several chins. His gray skin looked waxy.

"This the one who died from cirrhosis of the liver?" Kai asked Bean.

"This is what you dragged me all the way here to see!" Curtis practically bellowed. "Some fricken dead guy who died from drink? You think this is gonna scare me off booze. Who the hell do you think you are? If I want to drink myself to death, I got every fricken right to do it!"

He turned and stormed back toward the hall. Kai could see he'd made a mistake. "That's not what I brought you down here to see," he said.

"Screw you!" Curtis yelled.

"I swear."

"You can go to hell."

It was clear to Kai that nothing he could say would change the old man's mind. He turned and looked to Bean for help.

"There is something else," Bean said, reaching for the door to the dressing room.

Curtis paused and studied him.

"This you really will want to see," Bean said, reaching into the room and flicking on the light.

Curtis stepped to the doorway and peeked in. "Oh, my lord," he mumbled.

Eighteen

You would have thought Curtis had just found a long lost brother. He stepped close to the boards and ran his fingers over them, like he wasn't sure he could trust his eyes. The gratitude he was feeling seemed to spill out of him and fill the room. Kai would have sworn the place warmed up a few degrees.

"There's one we lost," he said.

"The Yater." Curtis had already noticed. "It's okay, grom. Believe me, it's more than okay." He stood there among the caskets and stared at his boards for a long time. Then he turned to Kai and Bean. "How?"

Kai shook his head. "Doesn't matter."

"Does to me," Curtis said. "You know who took them?"

"Not quite."

Curtis frowned. "Then how'd you find them? Aw, forget it. You don't want to tell me, you don't have to. You boys want to give me a hand gettin' them back to my place?"

"Not just yet," Kai said.

"Huh?"

"We still need 'em for something," Kai said. "But I promise you will get them back soon."

"You realize these are my boards, and if I want 'em I can take 'em right now?" Curtis asked.

"I wouldn't," Kai said. "Really, old man, it's important."

A crooked smile appeared on Curtis's face. "Boy, you are some piece of work. Okay, I guess since you got these boards back, it behooves me to let you play with 'em a bit longer."

Curtis backed out of the room and Bean turned off the light. Kai thought they were going to head back up the stairs, but Curtis went toward the embalming room and stopped a few feet away from the stiff lying on the embalming table.

"What'd he really die of?" he asked.

Bean went over to the table. "I don't remember what they said, but I doubt it was a disease like cirrhosis or cancer. Those ones usually waste away. This guy looks like he went pretty fast. Since there's no visible trauma, if I had to guess, I'd go with a heart attack. Although a stroke or aneurysm is always a possibility."

"How about suicide?" Curtis asked.

Bean gave the body a closer look, then shook his head. "I've only seen a few. It's a funny thing, but they never look like they're at peace, even here. See how peaceful this guy looks?"

"Yeah." Curtis rubbed his palm along his grizzled jaw. "Son of a gun not only looks peaceful, he looks younger than me."

Bean picked up a blue folder and opened it. "Sixty-three."

"Hell, that's ten years older," Curtis grumbled.

Kai was tempted to suggest that maybe the stiff had been kinder to his body over the years, but he quickly thought better of it. Curtis would no doubt come to the same conclusion.

"Well, may he rest in peace," Curtis said.

"Actually, he's going to rest in a six-thousand-dollar Persian bronze continuous-weld casket with swing bar hardware, champagne velvet interior and locking mechanism," Bean read.

"Locking mechanism?" Curtis raised an eyebrow. "In case he decides he wants out?"

"Or someone wants in," Bean said, closing the folder. "There are some pretty strange folks out there."

"I think I've seen—and heard—enough." Curtis started for the stairs.

Kai held the back door open for the older man.

"You staying here tonight?" Curtis asked.

Kai nodded.

"It's always nice to have another live body around," Bean joked. "Keeps things balanced."

"Son, I always thought you were a bit strange, but now you're bordering on scary," Curtis said.

"We couldn't have gotten those boards back without him," Kai said.

"Then let me shake your hand." Curtis started to offer his hand, then stopped. "You didn't, uh, touch our friend down there, did you?"

"Never without gloves," Bean said.

"Okay." Curtis and Bean shook hands. "Thanks, Bean. You don't know how much it means to me."

"No sweat," said Bean.

Curtis turned to Kai. "And thank you, grom."

"Think you can make it back to the motel okay?" Kai asked.

"I ain't dead yet." Curtis left, and Kai and Bean went up to Bean's apartment. Bean put on a CD. "Why do I suddenly think that not giving Curtis back the boards has something to do with getting the proof that Big Dave was the one who took them?"

"Uh, maybe 'cause you're smart?" Kai guessed.

"There's just one thing we must agree on, my friend," Bean said. "We are not going to have a parade of people coming through this place to look at those boards, got it? My parents will throw a total fit. Curtis was the last one."

Kai nodded. He'd noticed on Bean's desk a copy of the entry form for the Northeast Championship and picked it up.

"What do you think?" Bean asked.

Kai shrugged. "Can't decide, but something weird happened at Pete's tonight. Lucas said his father will pay for me to enter."

"What a jerk," Bean said.

"Lucas or Buzzy?" Kai asked.

"Buzzy," said Bean. "Don't you see? Buzzy's doing a head trip on his own son."

"Lucas knows why he's doing it," Kai said. "He's trying to get him motivated."

"Okay, but if Lucas isn't that motivated to begin with, doesn't that tell you something?" Bean replied.

He had a good point. One that Kai had suspected was true all along.

"You want to know who's really motivated?" Kai said. "Spazzy."

"He wants to enter?" Bean asked, surprised.

"Yeah."

"You tell him this is going to be a little different than Fairport?"

"I tried," Kai said.

Nineteen

The next morning Bean and Kai woke up before dawn. A little while later, downstairs in the lot behind the funeral home, the air actually had a nip to it.

"Feel that?" Bean said.

"Fall," said Kai. "Won't be long before we're back in wet suits."

"Yeah, but fall's also when we get those good offshore breezes," Bean said. "We'll get some nice open-faced waves today."

They got in the hearse and headed for the beach. It was still dark when they parked in the lot.

"You ever get that parking permit?" Kai asked as they got out of the hearse.

"Better believe it," Bean said. "Know what else I realized about these parking meters? I bet a lot of people won't mind running up and down the beach all day the first or second time, but when you have to do it every day, not only is it a royal pain to go back and forth, but it starts to be real money after a while. And you constantly have to go around looking for quarters."

"Unless you're a resident of the town or staying in one of those fancy resorts that'll give out temporary permits," Kai said.

"Exactly," Bean said as they unloaded their boards from the back. "You were right, Kai. It's just another form of harassment against anyone who isn't rich."

The faintest hint of light was beginning to show in the east as they walked across the boardwalk and stepped onto the cool sand.

"How far into the fall do you usually surf?" Kai asked.

"Sometimes the first week of December," Bean answered. "I've got a pretty heavy wet suit with a hood, and I'll come out on any sunny day that gets over forty-five degrees. By Christmas the water's just too cold, no matter how warm the day gets."

Christmas, Kai thought. It was hard to imagine where he'd be by then.

With the sky in the east slowly brightening, they stopped near the tide mark and looked at the beach.

"Not nearly as many jellyfish this morning," Bean said.

"The waves aren't bad either," Kai said. The better sets were around chest high, breaking smoothly against the offshore breeze.

He and Bean put their boards down on the sand and started to wax them. They were strapping on their leashes when Lucas and Everett came down the beach. Lucas was carrying a board. Everett had a tripod on his shoulder.

"Everett's gonna record us so we can compare what we're doing," Lucas said.

"You'd rather film than surf?" Kai asked Everett.

"Hey, this could be valuable footage someday," Everett said. "'Lucas Frank and Kai Herter, the Early Years.'"

Kai and Lucas picked up their boards, hit the water, and started to paddle out. Bean, on his long board, was ahead of them. The sky continued to brighten in the east.

"Hey, I meant to tell you about something I read in this book about the history of surfing," Lucas said as they paddled.

"Is it about Duke Kahanamoku being a competitive swimmer?" Kai asked. "Because that doesn't mean he was or would have been a competitive surfer."

"No, this goes back way before his time," Lucas said. "Back to some of the first accounts of Hawaiians by white visitors. Here's the news. Even back then Hawaiians competed in surfing. They made bets and surfed to see who won."

"What's your point?" Kai asked.

"Maybe competition is just a natural thing," Lucas said. "It makes it fun."

"You find competing fun?" Kai asked.

"Sometimes," Lucas said.

"And what about when it's not fun?" Kai asked.

"Look, dude, all I'm saying is maybe it's a choice each person makes," Lucas said. "There's no right or wrong about it."

"That's what I've been saying all along," Kai said.

"You sure?" asked Lucas. "'Cause most of the time it seems to me that you're saying competition is just plain wrong."

"Only when it messes up the surfing for everyone else," Kai said.

They got outside. Bean paddled beyond them. Being on a long board he could catch the waves earlier, and as the next set started to come in, that's exactly what he did, riding backside past Kai and Lucas with only his shoulders and head visible from behind.

The next wave was up for grabs, and Kai was actually surprised when Lucas nodded at him and said, "You or me?" But then Kai thought he understood. This was what Buzzy wanted. Whatever Kai did, Lucas would watch and try to do better. So be it, but Kai had no intention of showing his best moves so soon. He took off, did a big bottom turn, followed by two straight up, frontside snaps, followed by a floater. Having never been videoed surfing before, he couldn't help looking up to see if Everett really had the digital camcorder on him. That took his attention off the wave just long enough for him to catch a rail and bite it. But it hardly mattered. The ride was over anyway.

Behind him Lucas took off on a nearly identical wave, and tried to do the same combination of moves. It was hard for Kai to tell how well he'd done, but with Everett now recording Lucas, the truth would be on the screen.

Lucas stayed with the wave longer than Kai had and then came to shore to watch the video. Bean had already gone in, curious to see what Everett had filmed. Kai went in as well. All three left their boards on the sand and headed for Everett. They crowded around the tripod.

"Okay," Bean announced. "Let's go to the videotape!"

"You mean, digital replay," Everett corrected him.

They peered into the small viewing screen on the camcorder and watched Kai's ride. Having never seen himself on a screen before, Kai was pleasantly surprised. Although by now he should have known better, he'd always had a secret fear that somehow he didn't really look like a surfer, that anyone who watched him would see right away that there was something different, or not quite right, about the way he surfed. But as far as he could tell, he looked just like everyone else.

Bean provided the narration. "Kai Herter takes a late drop in order to maximize his speed. Skims down the face into a powerful bottom turn. Notice no loss of velocity as he turns back up, gets nearly horizontal, nice frontside snap. Back down, then up into a second frontside snap. Into a floater. Suddenly remembers he's being filmed. Looks up to make sure the camera has caught this stellar ride, forgets that he's in the middle of a floater, screws up, gets hammered. Reasonably good ride until he forgot he was a surfer and became a movie star instead."

Kai and the others chuckled, both because it was funny, and because it was true.

"Hey, what's going on?"

They turned and found Spazzy, in a sweatshirt and trunks, twitching as he put down his board and joined them.

"Look who got out of jail," Kai said, slapping him on the shoulder. "How'd you do it?"

Spazzy grinned sheepishly. "You'll love this. I got up real early and went down to the beach in front of our house and cleared out every jellyfish in sight. Then I went back in and got Jillian and showed her how the tide must have changed and all the jellyfish were gone."

"Well, you're half right," Bean said. "There aren't nearly as many as there were yesterday."

"So what are you guys up to?" Spazzy asked, nodding at Everett's tripod and digital camcorder.

"We're comparing the surfing performance of Kai and Lucas," Everett explained.

"Cool!" Spazzy said. "Can I watch?"

"Sure, dude," Kai said.

"We just did Kai's ride," Everett said. "Okay, now here's Lucas on pretty much the same size wave."

They watched on the screen as Lucas took off on his wave. Only he caught it earlier and a little farther out on the shoulder. This time Bean didn't narrate, either because he wasn't sure how Lucas would react, or because he could see from the start that Lucas's ride wouldn't be as good as Kai's. Starting earlier, Lucas wasn't able to generate the speed Kai had. He made a good bottom turn, but didn't get nearly as horizontal on the way back up. His backside snap was okay, but didn't leave him with enough juice for a second so he crouched down, generating more speed and a couple more turns, pushing the ride for length.

"That's it." Everett turned off the camera to save the batteries for the next session. Lucas was quiet. Kai knew he couldn't be happy with what he'd just seen.

"Well, that sucked," Lucas finally said. "I'm gonna have to take off deeper in the curl if I'm gonna have any kind of chance." Without another word he went back to his board, picked it up, and headed out. At the water's edge he stopped and looked back at Kai. "You coming?"

"In a second," Kai said. He turned back to Bean, Spazzy, and Everett. "Interesting, huh?"

"I hate to say it, but it looks like Buzzy was right," Bean said. "Without you there to compare his ride to, it would have been harder for him to see what was possible on that wave." He looked at Spazzy. "You coming in?"

"In a second," Spazzy said, and started to wax his board.

"You sure you want to keep doing this?" Everett asked Kai once Lucas was out of earshot.

"Why not?" Kai asked.

"Lucas is a plugger," Everett said. "He'll keep at it until he figures out how you do it, and how he can do it just as well."

"So?"

"What Everett's trying to say is if you do decide to enter the Northeast Championship, it's gonna be a lot harder to beat Lucas if he knows all your moves," Bean said.

Kai shrugged. "If he wins, then he deserves it."

"Hey, what about me?" Spazzy asked, in a way that made it hard to know whether he was joking or not.

"If you win, then you deserve it," Kai said.

"No, I meant, you guys think I could get filmed, too?"

Kai looked at Everett, who nodded. "No problem. I've got plenty of memory."

"Great. Thanks!" Spazzy started to strap on his leash.

"See you out there." Kai got his board and paddled back outside where Lucas was waiting for him. By now Spazzy was about halfway out as well.

"He coming out here too?" Lucas asked, obviously unhappy.

"You have to ask?" Kai replied.

"You sure have a strange collection of friends," Lucas said.

"I think that depends on your point of view," Kai replied.

Lucas didn't answer.

Twenty

Lucas and Kai kept riding waves and study
ing the videos. Everett was right about Lucas.
What he lacked in talent he made up for
with repetition and determination. Kai had to
push himself to stay ahead of the guy. As the
morning progressed and they went for harder
and harder stunts and turns, the wipeouts
increased. Kai found himself getting more
tired than usual.

"Man, I don't know what would make a
better show," Everett said at one point. "The
rides you guys are getting or the wipeouts."

Spazzy gamely tried to keep up with
them, but everyone knew he was out of his
league. When they watched their rides on the

camcorder, he always waited for Kai and Lucas to head back out before he asked Everett if he could see his.

By now the sun was growing hot and the beach was getting crowded. Sam, Derek, and Runt showed up, and they all wanted Everett to record their rides as well. Curious kids came around, bugging Everett and wanting to know what was going on. Booger and Shauna arrived. The waves at Screamers started to feel crowded.

At one point, after waiting what felt like forever for a decent set, Kai paddled into a wave only to have Booger drop in on him. Kai had to bail and paddle back outside, where Lucas waited with a smug look on his face. "Still want this break to be open to everyone?" he asked.

Kai sighed. He was not thrilled.

Meanwhile someone in the water must have told Booger that he'd dropped in on Kai because when he paddled back out, he was filled with apologies.

"I'm sorry, dude," he said. "I know I screwed up. I just didn't see you."

"It's cool, Boogs," Kai said.

Shauna paddled over to them. "I think I'll go over to Sewers. It's too crowded here."

"Just as crowded over at Sewers," Booger pointed out. "Only it's all spongeheads. And you know how they have no respect at all for surfers." He winked at Kai.

"Welcome to August in Sun Haven," Bean mumbled.

"I still like my chances at Sewers," Shauna said, and started to paddle over there.

"Guess I'll go with you," Booger said. "At least then Kai won't have to worry about me getting in his way again."

Kai hated to admit it, but he wasn't sorry to see Screamers get a little less crowded. Bobbing on his long board, it was almost as if Bean could read his thoughts. "Know what?" he said. "Sometimes things look better on paper than they do in real life."

"I bet September around here is just awesome with all the tourists gone and the kids back in school," Kai said.

Bean looked at Spazzy. "Hey, dude, why don't we go over to Sewers too? Might be fun to run over some bodyboarders."

"No, I gotta stay here," Spazzy answered. "This is where the contest is gonna be held, and the more wave time I get, the better my chances."

Bean gave Kai a look that said, *"Well, I tried."*

Kai nodded to show he appreciated the effort. He really didn't mind Spazzy surfing Screamers. He just didn't want to see the kid be totally disappointed at the Northeast Championship.

They surfed until around 11 A.M. By then the winds had turned onshore and were kicking up whitecaps. Kai and the others had been in the water for nearly five hours, and they were tired and hungry. As the waves started to get blown out, one by one or in pairs, the surfers came in until only Spazzy was left out there.

"What's he doing?" Bean asked Kai as they wrapped their leashes around the tails of their boards.

"He's been out there a long time," Everett said. "He's got to be tired."

"He's smart enough to know when to come in," Kai said.

Everyone headed up to Pete's Hubba Hubba for lunch. As usual, Kai and his friends sat at their regular table and Lucas and his brahs sat at theirs. Today Everett chose to sit with Lucas.

"Am I the only one who thinks it's kind of strange that we've gotten to the point where we can share the same surf break, but still can't eat together?" Bean asked.

"You really want to eat with Runt?" Booger whispered, which made most of the people at Kai's table grin.

"Good point, Boogs," Bean said. "Maybe some things are better left the way they are."

Kai noticed that Deb Hollister, Lucas's pretty blond, older girlfriend, had arrived on the terrace. He realized he'd never seen her around during the day before, and wondered if she had some kind of summer job. He expected her to go over to Lucas's table and was more than a little surprised when she came toward him and his friends instead.

"Did you bring them?" Shauna asked.

Deb nodded.

"Great." Shauna got up, and she and Deb headed over to Lucas's table.

"What's going on?" Booger asked. "Did she bring what?"

They watched while Deb opened her bag and handed some small blue envelopes to Shauna, who gave one to each of the brahs. Then Shauna and Deb came over to Kai's table and did the same thing. Kai and his friends quickly tore open the envelopes.

Inside was an invitation:

SURPRISE!
Jillian Winthrop, Shauna McNeale
and Deborah Hollister
invite you to an end-of-
the-summer pool party
in honor of
Caleb "Spazzy" Winthrop.
Bring bathing trunks
and a good attitude
AND DON'T TELL SPAZZY!
RSVP

"What's 'RSVP' mean?" Booger asked.

"It means you should let them know if you're coming to the party or not," Bean explained.

"Rizvipuh?" Booger tried to pronounce it.

"No, doofus, it stands for *répondez s'il vous plâit,*" Bean explained. "That's French."

Booger turned to Kai. "Did you know that?"

Kai shook his head.

"So I guess the answer's yes, huh?" Booger said.

"I don't think that's a problem at this

table," Kai said, subtly nodding his head toward Lucas and his brahs. Over at Lucas's table almost everyone had a scowl on his face as if he had no idea what to do. Runt ripped up his invitation and tossed the pieces in the air.

"I guess that's one way of RSVP-ing," Bean said.

"Not that Spazzy would care," said Booger.

Spazzy . . . Kai looked around. "Where is he, anyway?"

The words were hardly out of his mouth when he noticed a commotion down on the beach, and the distant wail of sirens approaching.

Kai jumped out of his chair and charged toward the crowd on the beach. A couple of mothers were leading small children away from the scene, moving them along like there was something they did not want the youngsters to see. Kai weaved and slipped through the mob until the bodies became too tightly packed. He turned to a potbellied tourist with bright red shoulders and a gleaming bald head.

"What's everyone looking at?" Kai asked anxiously.

"Some surfer kid drowned," the man answered.

Spazzy . . . In the background the sirens

were getting louder. Kai started to push and shove through the mass of bodies. The people around him didn't like it. "Hey, where do you think you're going?" "Say 'excuse me.'" "Back off!"

Kai had no intention of backing off. He forced his way to the center of the crowd. Several lifeguards were kneeling in the sand, blocking so much of the body lying on its back that it was hard at first to know if it was Spazzy. One lifeguard was giving him mouth-to-mouth resuscitation while another straddled the body, administering sharp thrusts just below his rib cage.

Kai prayed that it wasn't Spazzy. Whomever it was lay as listless and lifeless on the sand as the corpses in Bean's basement.

The sirens were loud now.

"Look out!" "Coming through!" The crowd parted as a group of paramedics fought through the throng, carrying a stretcher and bright orange first aid kits. Kai caught bits and pieces of the hurried, anxious conversation between the lifeguards and paramedics. . . . "Not responding." "Not breathing." "Can't find a pulse."

A small green tank of oxygen appeared,

along with a clear plastic mask. Kai caught a glimpse of Spazzy's unconscious face, eyes closed, hair matted down, sand covering one cheek. One of the paramedics pulled a thin, limp arm toward him, swabbed it with a cotton ball and injected something.

"Get him up!" "Let's go." The paramedics and lifeguards lifted the stretcher with Spazzy on it and rushed toward the boxy ambulance with wide knobby tires for traction in the sand. With the paramedics still performing CPR, they lifted the stretcher into the back. The doors slammed shut, the siren wailed, the tires spun, digging ruts and kicking up rooster tails of sand as the ambulance sped away.

The crowd began to scatter, going back to their umbrellas and beach towels. Kai stared at the impression in the sand where his friend had lain. A dozen feet away, Spazzy's board lay upside down on the sand.

He felt an arm go around his shoulder. It was Bean. Suddenly Kai had a thought. "You have to call Jillian."

"Already did," Bean said. "Let's get our stuff and go to the hospital."

Kai didn't budge. He felt as if the universe were collapsing in on him.

"Come on, dude. There's nothing to do here."

"There was just one thing I was supposed to do," Kai said. "Just one stupid little thing. I was supposed to keep an eye on him."

Twenty-one

They collected Spazzy's board and then headed up the beach and across the boardwalk. In the parking lot they were putting their boards in the back of the hearse when Booger and Shauna showed up with stricken, worried expressions.

"We heard it was a surfer," Shauna said.

"There was no one else out there except Spazzy," said Booger.

"It was him," Kai said, finding it difficult to meet their gazes.

"Did you see him?" Shauna asked.

Kai nodded.

"How was he?"

Kai couldn't look her in the eye.

"Oh, no!" Shauna gasped, and turned to Bean.

"It's not good," Bean said. "We're going to the hospital if you want to come."

"I'm going," Booger said. "Just let me go get my stuff." He looked at Shauna. "I'll get your board too."

"Thanks, Boogs." Shauna turned to Bean. "Can I use your cell phone?"

Bean handed it to her, and she started to call the kids she knew who worked at Ice Cream to see if someone could fill in for her that afternoon.

While they waited for Booger, Kai sat down on the curb and felt the hot sun on his head. Bean sat down next to him, his knees and elbows jutting out. "How're you doing?" he asked.

Kai shook his head. His mind was a jumble of fragments from past and present, like shards of newly broken glass mixed in with dull, smooth pieces from the sea. *Getting hurt surfing. Lifeguards. Stretchers. Cars. Accidents. Hospitals. People dying.* It had all happened before. It was all happening again. It was difficult for him to put his thoughts together in any kind of sensible way.

"It's not your fault," Bean whispered, so Shauna wouldn't hear.

Kai felt a shadow over him. He looked up to find Everett and Lucas. Derek, Sam, and Runt were behind them. Runt was holding some paper napkins over his nose. The napkins were spotted with red.

"What do you hear?" Lucas asked.

"We don't know yet," Bean said.

"Someone said he wasn't breathing when they put him in the ambulance," Everett said. "I don't think anyone really knows."

Booger came back with his bodyboard and Shauna's surfboard and Bean helped him put them in the back of the hearse. Shauna snapped Bean's cell phone closed.

"I can't find anyone to fill in for me," she said, handing the phone back to Bean. "Guess I have to go to work."

"We'll let you know as soon as we hear anything," Bean said. He turned to the others. "We're heading over to the hospital."

Kai hadn't budged from the curb. He'd heard everything they'd said, but the words lacked meaning and sense. He felt someone touch him on the shoulder and looked up to see Bean. "Come on, dude. Let's go."

Booger was already in the front seat of the hearse. Kai got in next to him and closed the passenger door. Outside Lucas and his brahs were drifting away, except for Everett, who was talking to Bean. Then Bean went around the front of the car and got in the driver's seat.

He started the hearse and backed out of the parking space.

"Just drive safely," Kai heard himself say. Bean gave him a strange look, as if wondering what would prompt him to say that. Kai knew exactly why he'd said it, but it wasn't something he could, or would, explain. Bean drove quickly, but not recklessly.

"What happened to Runt?" Booger asked.

"I asked Everett," Bean said. "Seems he said something really stupid about Spazzy and got clocked for it."

"By Everett?" Booger asked.

Bean shook his head. "Lucas."

Sun Haven Hospital was just outside of town. It was in the process of being expanded and Bean had to weave around a lot of construction vehicles and temporary barriers before they found a place to park near the emergency entrance.

Still clad in their damp trunks, Kai, Bean,

and Booger went into the emergency room waiting area. Jillian and Marta, the house-keeper, were already there. They both looked pale and had red-rimmed eyes.

Bean went over to them. Kai and Booger followed.

"Heard anything?" Bean asked.

"They're working on him," Jillian said.

"Nothing else?" Bean asked.

Jillian shook her head and started to cry. Marta put her arm around her and looked up at the boys. "The doctor said she'll tell us when there is news."

Bean turned to Kai and Booger. "You guys want to stay, right?"

Kai nodded. They sat down.

Half an hour passed. Bean's cell phone rang. As he answered it, a nurse behind the desk waved at him and pointed at a sign on the wall that said cell phone use was prohibited. Bean went outside for a while, then came back in. He sat down with Kai and Booger, bent forward, and spoke in a low voice: "That was Shauna. She said a couple of spongeheads just came into Ice Cream. They were out body-boarding at Screamers and saw what happened to Spazzy. They said it looked like he was trying to catch some white water in and a wave broke on top of him."

"But that happens all the time," Booger whispered back.

"Yeah, but they said afterward Spazzy seemed to have a really hard time getting back on his board. Like he'd cramped up or something. Next thing they knew, the board was just floating there and no Spazzy."

"Huh?" Booger didn't get it.

"Because he was underwater," Kai guessed.

Bean nodded. "I'm gonna go tell Jillian. I think she'd want to know."

He got up. Kai sat with his elbows on his knees and his chin propped in his hands and waited while Bean spoke to Jillian. Their talk seemed to go on a lot longer than Kai had expected, but he didn't think much of it until Jillian came over to him.

Kai looked up, truly surprised to see her.

"It's not your fault," she said.

Kai blinked. Now he knew why Bean had spoken to her for so long.

"I promised I'd watch him," Kai said. "He said the one thing his teacher in California insisted on was that he always have someone there with him."

"It wasn't your responsibility," said Jillian.

"I promised. I just forgot."

"That's understandable," Jillian said. "When my brother was out there on the board, he was just like everyone else. It was easy to forget about his condition."

Kai hung his head. It was nice of her to say these things, and he sensed that she really meant it. But it didn't make any difference.

"Kai?" Jillian said, and waited for him to look at her again. "This was the best summer my brother ever had. It was the happiest I've ever seen him. Ever. It couldn't have happened without you. I will always be grateful to you for doing the one thing no one else was ever able to do. You made him feel just like everyone else."

Kai nodded. He knew she meant every word of it.

But if Spazzy didn't make it, it wouldn't matter.

Twenty-two

Twenty minutes later a small woman with short curly black hair and red-framed glasses came into the waiting room. She was wearing a white medical jacket, and a black stethoscope hung around her neck. Jillian jumped up to meet her, with Marta, Kai, Bean, and Booger close behind.

"He's awake and breathing on his own," the doctor announced with a smile.

Jillian breathed an audible sigh of relief, then collapsed into Bean's arms and began to sob. "Thank God!"

"He's going to be okay?" Kai asked.

"I think so," the doctor said. "It was touch and go there for a while, but I've seen cases like this before, and thanks to the quick response by the lifeguards and EMS, we're hoping he got enough oxygen to prevent any brain damage. Of course we're going to want to keep him here for a day or two to make sure."

"Can we see him?" Jillian asked, rubbing the tears out of her reddened eyes.

The doctor looked around at the small group. "He's been through a difficult experience, and he's very weak and tired. Maybe just one family member today. We can talk about more visitors tomorrow if he still needs to stay."

With no doubt who the one family member would be, Jillian went inside with the doctor while Kai and the others returned to their waiting room seats. Out of the corner of his eye, Kai watched Marta remove a small white ball of tissues from her bag and dab her eyes.

Bean shook his head. No one could talk for a moment. It had been too fricken close.

Kai nodded silently. He felt as if he'd been given a once-in-a-lifetime reprieve from bad luck. Maybe not everything had to go bad all the time. He nudged Bean with his elbow. "Can I use your phone?"

"Oh, right. Shauna." Bean handed him the phone, and Kai went outside and called Ice

Cream. He wasn't surprised that Shauna answered on the first ring. Kai could hear music and voices in the background, as if the ice cream shop was crowded.

"Hello?" she asked anxiously.

"He's all right," Kai said.

"Kai? Oh, God, thanks for calling." Shauna sounded incredibly relieved. "What did they say?"

"He's conscious and breathing on his own."

"Did you see him?"

"Maybe tomorrow."

"That is such good news," Shauna said. "I hope you feel better too."

"Just really lucky and happy," Kai said. "If it happened to me again I—" He caught himself and stopped.

"If what happened to you again?" Shauna asked.

"Nothing."

For a moment there was silence on the phone. Kai imagined that Shauna was debating whether to push the question.

"It's really busy here now," she said. "You coming back into town?"

"Yeah."

"Promise you'll stop by?"

"Okay. See you soon." Kai snapped the phone shut, went back into the emergency room waiting area.

Booger and Bean were talking quietly so Marta wouldn't hear. "You think Jillian'll ever let Spazzy surf again?"

"I think the real question is whether *we'll* ever let him surf again," Bean replied in a whisper.

For the first time in hours, Kai felt a smile on his face. "Not alone. That's for sure."

A little while later Jillian came back into the waiting room looking pale and drained, but strangely cheerful at the same time. Kai and his friends got to their feet.

"How is he?" Kai asked.

"Tired, like the doctor said. They gave him something to calm him down, so he was drowsy. But he actually sounded okay."

"Did he say what happened?"

"He thinks he got a cramp in his leg, and then accidentally inhaled some water," Jillian said. "He doesn't remember anything after that. The doctor said they couldn't believe how much water came out of him."

"Not to mention a jellyfish or two," Bean quipped.

"He wanted me to tell you that he's sorry," Jillian said.

"For what?" Kai asked.

"For staying out when the rest of you went in. He said he knew he shouldn't have done it, and that the waves were no good anyway."

"I guess it just shows how much he loves surfing," Kai said.

"He also said something about wanting to enter another contest," Jillian said. "Do you know what he was talking about?"

Kai, Bean, and Booger glanced at one another. Kai knew what they were all thinking. Two hours ago the kid practically drowned, and already he was talking about going back out.

"We can talk him out of it, if you want," Kai offered.

"Thanks." Jillian paused for a moment. "To tell you the truth, I can't even begin to think about that right now. First I have to make sure he's okay."

Outside, Jillian and Marta went to their car and drove home. Kai noticed that the wind had picked up, and swirling gusts blew papers and sandy dust around them. In the sky, dark gray clouds were approaching quickly. The air had an unusual scent and felt as if it was lightly charged with electricity.

"Looks like the mother of all thunderstorms is coming," Bean said as he, Kai, and Booger got back into the hearse. Bean was just about to start the car when his cell phone rang. He flipped it open and looked at the display and frowned. "No idea who this is," he said as he brought the phone to his ear and answered. "Hello? . . . Oh, yeah . . . No, it's cool. . . . No, he's gonna be okay. . . . Yeah . . . Right . . . See ya later."

Bean flipped the phone closed. "You'll never guess."

Kai and Booger exchanged a puzzled look.

"Lucas," Bean said. "He wanted to know about Spazzy."

"How'd he get your cell phone number?" Booger asked.

"Called the funeral home and got it from my mom," Bean said.

"Wow, I never would've expected that," Booger said.

Bean drove out of the hospital parking lot. "Dudes, this is a day we won't forget for a while."

"You're telling me," said Kai.

"What do you guys want to do now?" Booger asked.

"I promised Shauna I'd stop by Ice Cream," Kai said.

"Is it okay if I drop you off?" Bean asked. "I'd just as soon not be driving around when this storm hits."

"No problem," Kai said.

"I'll see you later?" Bean asked.

"If it's okay," Kai said.

"Hey, *mi casa es su casa*," Bean said.

"Is that like RSVP?" Booger asked.

Bean groaned.

Huge drops of water were starting to splat against the hearse's windshield when Bean dropped Kai off at Ice Cream. Kai could hear booms of thunder in the distance. The normally crowded Main Street was almost empty, and the few tourists and vacationers who were still out were scurrying for shelter.

Boom! Kai was pushing through the doorway of Ice Cream when the sudden crack of thunder made him jump. The lights in the shop flickered. Inside, a woman eating an ice cream cone gasped loudly, and a couple of little kids began to cry. Outside, the rain began to roar down in light gray sheets of liquid that made it almost impossible to see across the street.

Kai went up to the counter. On the other side, Shauna was struggling to get her ice cream scoop through a pail of dark chocolate ice cream. When she saw Kai, she stopped.

"What was it like at the hospital?"

"Scary until the doctor came out and said he was okay."

"Thank God," Shauna said again.

"Jillian said he's already talking about the Northeast Championship."

Shauna shook her head and rolled her eyes. "Sometimes I think there's something wrong with all of us."

"If there is, I hope it's something good," Kai said.

"Ahem." A chubby man standing at the counter cleared his throat loudly.

"Your cone is coming, sir," Shauna said with forced cheer, and started to dig through the chocolate again.

"You're going to have strong arms by the time summer's over," Kai said.

"I keep wondering if it'll help my paddling," Shauna said. She finished the chocolate cone. "Here you are, sir."

The man paid for his cone. Thanks to the heavy rain, no new customers had entered the shop. "Your regular?" Shauna asked Kai.

"Uh, sure, thanks."

Shauna turned away to dip the scoop in warm water. At that moment someone stopped under the awning outside Ice Cream to get out of the rain. It was Jade, in a rain-soaked white T-shirt that left nothing to the imagination. With one arm pressed against herself in an almost fruitless attempt at modesty, she peered through the window, saw Kai inside, and waved.

"Be right back," Kai said to Shauna, and went out to join her under the awning.

"Looks like you got caught in the rain," he said, using every ounce of willpower to keep his eyes from drifting where they weren't supposed to go.

"Just my luck," said Jade. With her free hand she tried to fluff out her rain-flattened short black hair. "So I heard what happened. Is your friend okay?"

"Looks like it," Kai said. "Thanks to the lifeguards and EMS."

"That's good," Jade said. "We've had surfers drown here before. Usually when they go out in storm surf and their leashes snap or they get hit in the head by the board. It's such a night-mare. You just hate hearing about it."

Kai nodded. The rain had let up slightly, but torrents of water coursed down the sides of the street and flooded the storm sewers.

"So you know that secret you wanted me to get Big Dave to reveal?" Jade asked.

"Yes?"

"He told me."

"Wow, thanks, Jade. You don't know how much that means to me. And how much it's going to mean to a lot of other people too."

"Wait a minute." Jade suddenly stiffened. "I'm telling *you*. No one else. And if you tell anyone I said it, I'll say that's not true. Don't forget. It's not only Big Dave's job that would be on the line. It would be mine, too. And I *need* that job."

Kai hadn't thought of that. "Okay, I understand."

"So I don't have to be nice to Big Dave anymore, right?" Jade asked.

"Well, maybe just a little longer," Kai said.

Jade made a face. "Why? He told us what you needed to know."

"Yeah, but if I want to keep you out of it, then I have to find another way to prove it," Kai said. "Can you give me a day to figure it out?"

Jade frowned. "You know, I wouldn't do this for anyone else."

"I'm just that irresistible, huh?"

"Don't kid yourself," Jade said. "No one is *that* irresistible. This is the last favor, okay? I really can't stand dealing with him."

"Gotcha."

Jade looked him straight in the eye. "And I'm getting a little tired of not dealing with you. I thought I was going to see you a little more often."

Kai swallowed slightly. "I hear you."

The rain continued to ease. With one arm still across her chest, Jade peeked out from under the awning. "Time to scoot." She gave him a quick kiss on the lips. "You owe me. Big-time."

Jade jogged off down the sidewalk. Kai went back into Ice Cream. Shauna was down at the far end of the shop, polishing the glass display case. She had a frown on her face and didn't look up when he came in. Kai waited for a moment. There was no vanilla cone with Reese's Pieces anywhere in sight, and Shauna was clearly ignoring him.

Kai turned around and left. Sometimes dealing with women was just a little too complicated.

Twenty-three

That night the storm blew through. The next morning Kai and Bean slept later than usual. The sun was already up when they got to the beach. The offshore breeze was crisp and cool. There was no doubt about fall coming. Kai wished he had a shorty wet suit, not so much because of the water temperature—it was still a comfortable seventy-two degrees—but because of the chill in the air.

Lucas was already in the water on his board. Once again Everett was setting up his camcorder.

The waves were perfect and chest high, clear blue-green under the cloudless sky. Tall plumes of rainbow spray peeled off the crests as they curled. You could have asked for a bigger day, but you couldn't have asked for a nicer one.

"Lucky you," Bean said with a yawn as he and Kai walked down the beach, their boards under their arms.

"What do you mean?" Kai asked.

"I guess I don't envy the idea of getting up each morning and finding Lucas waiting to hound you on the waves."

Kai shrugged. "It's only for the next few days. I'll survive."

They joined Everett on the dry side of the tide mark.

"Hey, I heard Spazzy's gonna be okay," Everett said. "That's great."

"Yeah."

"What a day, huh?" Everett asked.

"Wouldn't you rather be out there surfing?" Bean asked as he kneeled down and started to wax his board.

Everett shook his head. "I like surfing a lot, dude, but this is what I'm really into. Look at those waves. See how the breeze is holding the faces open just a second longer than usual? You see those faces and dream about what you can do on them with a board. I see those faces and dream about the extra footage I'll be able to get."

"You ever think about getting one of those waterproof cases, so you can shoot in the waves?" Kai asked.

"For sure," Everett said. "That's next on the list. Just gotta save up the money."

Bean finished waxing and picked up his board. "How's the jellyfish count?"

"Dropping," Everett said.

"Cool." He trotted toward the water.

Kai had purposely taken his time waxing this morning. Now that Bean was paddling out, he could speak to Everett alone. He had a special favor to ask him. Once Everett and Kai finished speaking, Kai paddled out and joined Lucas. As usual Bean was sitting farther outside on his long board.

"Anything new on your friend?" Lucas asked.

"Not since last night," Kai said. "Good news is they're pretty sure he's going to be okay. But it was close."

"Hard to believe," Lucas said.

"What do you mean?" Kai asked.

"That it happened here," Lucas said. "Who thinks of this as a dangerous break, you know? Pipeline, sure. Maverick's, of course. But Screamers in Sun Haven? It's like a joke."

Kai thought back to the night, a month ago, when he easily could have died in this very spot had it not been for Everett. Then again, he'd made an incredibly stupid mistake, surfing alone in big waves—at least for Sun Haven—and in the dark. "I guess we forget that it can happen almost anywhere."

"Guess so," Lucas said. He gestured into the distance, and Kai saw the dark lines of a new set approaching. "Ready?"

"Not quite," Kai said. "I want to enjoy one ride before it becomes work."

Lucas didn't reply. Kai spotted a promising wave and paddled over to catch it. He purposely took it early and out on the shoulder, did a lazy bottom turn, and then stayed in the face making nothing more than small adjustments and corrections to keep from outrunning the wave. Nothing showy. Nothing that would have earned a big score from any judge, but relaxing and enjoyable just the same. Long past the point where he should have kicked out, he stayed on the board, hopping it and fooling around, just because he didn't want the ride to end.

Lucas also caught a ride in that set, but Kai didn't see it. He only saw that Lucas was paddling back out at the same time he was. Soon they were both sitting outside again. Meanwhile Shauna and Sam had arrived separately and were waxing their boards.

"Ready?" Lucas sounded impatient.

Kai was tempted to ask what the rush was, but he thought he already knew the answer. Lucas was eager to get some hard charging in before the waves started to get crowded. Kai had agreed to be his sparring partner until the Northeast Championship, so it wasn't fair to give the guy grief.

"Sure," Kai said.

On the next wave Kai ripped, trying to force three or four moves into the space where he normally performed two. In a way it was sort of interesting to see how much you could pack into one ride. Kai could see the challenge. But he also saw how it could get old really fast.

They surfed and checked Everett's video for the rest of the morning. Now and then Bean joined them on the beach to watch. Shauna came out to Screamers, generally waiting for the others to catch waves before she took hers. Kai nodded at her a couple of times, but she ignored him, as if she was still angry from the night before. Derek arrived, and Kai couldn't help noticing how friendly and chatty she was with him.

By midmorning, when the onshore thermals started to blow the waves out, Kai was nearly exhausted. Being Lucas's sparring partner was hard work. But he couldn't say he hated it.

"Want to go see Spazzy?" Bean asked while they wrapped their leashes around the tails of their boards.

"Definitely," Kai said. He found himself glancing over at Shauna and Derek, who were sitting side by side on the sand looking out at the ocean.

"Interesting combination," Bean said. "Does it bother you?"

"You kidding?" Kai said. "No way."

They started up the beach. Lucas was reviewing his rides with Everett, but Kai had lost interest.

"Looks like Lucas is seriously gung ho about this contest," said Bean.

"Yeah, I noticed," Kai said.

"How's it feel to be his sparring partner?"

"Tiring," Kai said. "Every time I turn around he's right on my heels. I keep asking myself, Why am I doing this? Why would I want to do Buzzy Frank a favor?"

"Maybe you're enjoying it," Bean said. "A little competition can't hurt."

Kai winced inwardly. A little competition had once hurt him horribly. The scars on his leg were nothing compared to the scars inside.

They got to the parking lot. Each time Kai saw the hearse it reminded him of the tires Goldilocks had slashed. Kai didn't know what it had cost Bean to get all those tires replaced. He just knew it wasn't cheap. Of course, Bean, being the kind of guy he was, had never said a word about the money, but it still bothered Kai big-time.

"Hey, you weren't going without me, were you?" Shauna trotted up the beach carrying her board and slid it into the back of the hearse.

During the drive to the hospital Shauna sat between Bean and Kai. No one spoke. It was unusual for the three of them to be so quiet. Shauna didn't look in Kai's direction, and Kai didn't look in hers. Finally Bean said, "Nice waves today."

"Yes," said Shauna.

"You're catching more and more of them," said Bean.

"Thanks," Shauna said. "I had a couple of rides today that felt really good. Like I was going sideways right in front of the curl. But it's hard to stay there."

"It's about controlling your edge," Kai said. "You'll get it."

"I used to have this friend who took time to show me," Shauna said. "I don't know what happened to him."

"Ouch," Bean said, even though the comment had not been directed at him.

"Maybe your friend didn't know you still wanted help," Kai said.

"Or maybe he just got so distracted by tight bikinis and wet T-shirts that he forgot," Shauna said.

"Yeow, it's getting hot in here," said Bean.

"Maybe there's more going on than meets the eye," Kai said.

"All I know is, depending on where the eye looks there's already way too much to meet it," Shauna said. Both Kai and Shauna stared straight ahead as they spoke. Neither looked at the other.

"Time to get some fresh air in here." Bean

brought both windows down and let the breeze blow in.

"Hey, maybe it's my imagination," Kai said, "but it sort of looked like there might be other teachers interested in the job."

"Some surfers do manage to think about other people," Shauna said.

"Great, so then there's no problem," Kai said.

"Who ever said there was a problem?" Shauna asked, crossing her arms and staring straight ahead.

"Forget the fresh air." Bean brought the windows back up and reached for the dashboard. "This calls for AC."

They rode the rest of the way in silence. Bean parked in the main lot of Sun Haven Hospital. It was noon and they were inland where the sea breeze didn't reach. The blistering midday sun reminded Kai that while the first hints of fall might be creeping closer every morning and evening, the middle of the day still belonged to summer.

As they walked toward the main entrance, Bean pointed at the black Mercedes station wagon with the California plates. "Jillian's here." Inside they rode an elevator up to a brand-new pediatric wing. The light yellow walls were smooth with new paint and lined with brightly colored photographs. The floor was polished and glossy. Kai and his friends stopped at a nurses' station.

"Looks more like a NASA tracking station than a hospital," Bean said, pointing at the many computer terminals and monitors.

"If I ever get sick, this is definitely where I want to be," added Shauna.

A nurse directed them to Spazzy's room. The door was open. Inside, Spazzy was sitting up in bed, reading *Surfer* magazine. Jillian was sitting in a chair reading a book. When Bean knocked, they both looked up. To Kai it was hard to judge who had a bigger smile.

"Dudes!" Spazzy said. But despite his suntan, Kai thought he seemed pale underneath.

"Hey, man, waz up?" Bean held out his hand. Twitching and jerking, Spazzy managed to slap Bean's and Kai's palms. Shauna leaned over the bed and gave him a kiss on the cheek.

Spazzy actually blushed. "Hey, if girls are going to kiss me, I might try drowning more often!"

"Caleb, that is absolutely not funny," Jillian said sternly.

"Hate to say it, dude, but your sister's right," Kai agreed. "I mean, we were totally freaked yesterday."

"Okay, okay," Spazzy said. "Hey, want to hear something cool? The doctors said they've never seen a kid my size barf up so much seawater."

"Oh, Caleb," Jillian groaned.

"Any fish?" Bean asked.

"You mean sushi, don't you?" said Shauna.

"So what's the story with today?" Kai asked. "Know when they're going to let you go?"

"Any time now," Spazzy said. "We're just waiting around for the doctor to check me out. I'll be back in the water tomorrow morning."

"I beg your pardon," Jillian said.

"Aw, come on," Spazzy said. "I'm fine."

"Doctor Levine said he wants you to rest," Jillian said.

"Hey, what did I do last night?" Spazzy asked. "What am I doing today? What'll I do tonight? You know, too much rest can be bad for you."

Jillian rolled her eyes. "We'll see."

There was a single rap on the door, and a tall man in a white coat strode in. "So, how are we today, Caleb?"

"Hey, Doc, tell my sister I'll be okay to surf tomorrow," Spazzy said.

"Uh . . ." Caught by surprise, the doctor turned to Kai and his friends. "I think we'll need some privacy."

Bean, Shauna, and Kai understood. "We better take off," Bean said. "Catch you later."

They left the room and went back out into the hall, pulling the door closed behind them.

"Sounds like the old Spazzy is back," Shauna said.

"For sure," said Bean.

They walked back down the hall to the elevator. Bean pushed the button. While they waited, Kai noticed a large metal plaque on the wall. In raised bronze letters were the words "John Fraser Moncure Pediatric Wing," and under it were the names of various people on the hospital board, the architect who'd designed the wing, the construction company that had built it, and a long list of donors who'd contributed money to the venture. One name featured prominently on the hospital board and among the list of donors was Elliot "Buzzy" Frank.

A bell rang. Shauna stepped into the elevator. Bean held the door. "Kai?"

He joined them. The door shut and they started down.

"Something interesting on that plaque?" Bean asked.

"Guess who one of the major contributors to that new wing was?" Kai said.

Bean's forehead wrinkled. "Buzzy?"

"Good guess."

"Does that change your opinion of him?" Shauna asked.

"I don't know," Kai said. "But it's something to think about."

Twenty-four

They got into the hearse and headed back to Sun Haven. On Seaside Drive they found themselves behind an SUV with out-of-town plates, two thick silver board bags strapped to the roof, and dozens of surf stickers on the back window and bumper.

"The troops are coming," Bean said.

"Think you could drop me at Ice Cream?" Shauna asked. "It's almost time for me to start work."

"Sure." Bean checked his watch. "And I've got to get ready for a funeral."

"Driving?" Kai asked.

"Yeah. We've got a double header this

afternoon and one of the regular drivers is on vacation."

At Ice Cream Shauna got out and thanked Bean without even looking at Kai.

"Hey," Kai said as she started to turn away. Shauna stopped.

"I could try to help you with that edge stuff," Kai offered.

"I wouldn't want to waste any of your valuable time," Shauna replied.

"It's not so valuable," Kai said.

"Let's see tomorrow." Shauna headed across the sidewalk and into the shop.

"The wrath of Shauna," Bean said back in the hearse.

Kai shrugged.

"You know she's crazy about you," Bean said.

"She sure has a strange way of showing it," Kai said.

"Actually, pretty typical," Bean said. "You just have to know how to read the signs." They were headed down Main Street now. "Any place I can drop you?"

"Teddy's." Kai hoped she'd be in a better mood than the last time he'd seen her.

A few minutes later Bean stopped the

hearse beside the tall white picket fence.

"Thanks, Bean," Kai said as he got out.

"Catch you later?" Bean asked.

"Definitely," Kai said. He pushed the hearse's door closed and stepped onto Teddy's property, not sure whether to check the house or the workshop first. He decided to be optimistic and try the workshop. The whine of the power planer coming from the shaping room was a good sign. Kai went in, but stood outside the shaping room until he heard the power planer stop. Teddy didn't like to be disturbed when she was shaping. Kai knocked, then pushed open the door and stuck his head in.

Inside the shaping room Teddy was running her hand along the rail of a foam blank. She was wearing a respirator and covered with foam dust. The floor and just about every other flat surface was also covered with white dust. She shook the dust out of her hair and pulled off the respirator. "I was beginning to wonder if I'd ever see you again."

"After last time I wasn't sure you'd want to," Kai replied.

"Because I told you to get out? Listen, grommet, you want to work with me, you'll need a tougher hide than that."

Kai wasn't sure what to say. It sounded like they were working together again.

"So I heard you got that son of a bitch's boards back for him," she said, apparently referring to Curtis.

"How'd you hear that?" Kai asked, surprised.

"Things get around," Teddy said. "I like that. Means you get things done. You're not all talk, like most people around here."

"I could have told you that," Kai said, and winked.

Teddy chuckled. "I get it, you could have told me, but since most people are all talk, what difference would it have made? Very funny." Then she did something that *really* shocked him. "Come on, let's have a look at something." She went into the workshop. From a rack of finished, but unglassed boards, she pulled out the one he'd sketched the logo on. Kai was honestly surprised that she hadn't sanded the sketch off.

"It's not bad," she said.

"You serious?" Kai asked.

She tilted her forehead down and looked at him with a severe gesture. "Do I give out many compliments?"

"Actually, no," Kai said.

"Then when I do, you better take it seriously," she said. "Only, this is just a pencil sketch. I have no idea what it will look like colored in."

"I could color it," Kai offered.

"I'd rather you didn't use the actual board," Teddy said. "You wouldn't have any color sketches, would you?"

Kai did. Only they were back at T-licious. "I'd have to go get them."

Teddy gave him a funny look. "So?"

"So . . . what?" Kai replied, confused.

"So what the hell are you waiting for? Go get them," Teddy said, and went back into the shaping room, slamming the door behind her.

Twenty-five

As Kai walked into town he realized that he'd been purposefully avoiding T-licious ever since he'd stopped working there. Of all the places he could have gone, this was probably the one he wanted to see least. It was midafternoon now, and the sun was still hot and high overhead. The sidewalks were nearly empty. Almost everyone was at the beach or a pool. On Main Street an out-of-state minivan passed, loaded with boards in board socks. More competitors. Kai stopped across the street from the shop. There was hardly any trace left of the old custom T-shirt scam. Almost everything in the windows now was discount surf wear.

Kai took a deep breath and let it out

slowly. He could feel butterflies in his stomach. He would have preferred taking off on a twenty-five-footer at Maverick's to setting foot in that place again. Or maybe it wasn't setting foot in the shop that bothered him. Maybe it was having to ask the Alien Frog Beast for his sketches back.

He crossed the street, pushed open the door, and went in. Unlike the last time he'd been in the shop, the shelves and racks weren't bursting with merchandise. The knockoff sweatshirts on the shelves were piled only two or three high, and the garments displayed on the racks had empty hangers between them. Kai knew the signs. The end of August was here, and his father had no intention of restocking. Instead he planned to sell everything he could, and then take off leaving as many unpaid bills as possible.

Inside, his father was at his customary perch at the counter near the cash register, reading the newspaper and smoking a cigarette. When Kai came in, the Alien Frog Beast looked up and adjusted his square-framed glasses. "Well, well, look what the cat dragged in."

"How's it going?" Kai asked.

"Pretty good, actually," his father said. "Looks like we still did okay this summer, no thanks to that son of a bitch Buzzy Frank."

"Oh, right, the guy who actually made you pay your rent for once," Kai said, realizing too late that he'd made a mistake.

Pat's face hardened. "What do you want?"

"The color sketches I did for the logo you never used," Kai said.

"Why?"

"Someone wants to see them," said Kai.

"What for? They can't use that logo," Pat said.

"They just want to see what I can do."

Pat gazed at him for a moment silently and drummed his fingers against the glass counter. "I threw 'em out."

"Give me a break," Kai said. "You never throw anything out."

"Why should I give them to you?" his father asked.

"Maybe because I'm your son, and believe it or not, most fathers try to help their sons."

"What did you ever do for me?" the Alien Frog Beast asked.

"I worked for you for two years," Kai said.

"So?" his father said. "I put a roof over your head and fed you."

"Look," Kai said. "I never asked you for anything. I helped you with your scams. I'm sure I helped you make a lot of money that you've got stashed in safe-deposit boxes all over. All I'm asking for is a couple of sketches that you never wanted in the first place."

Pat glanced toward the back of the store. Kai wondered if he was making sure Sean wasn't listening. Then he motioned Kai closer. "Listen, that loser brother of yours isn't worth squat. At least you knew what to do without me having to tell you every damn little thing. Tell you what. You come back to work for me, and I'll make it worth your while. I'll give you a cut of the profits. Only you can't tell Sean, understand?"

Kai didn't understand. "Profits from this place?"

His father shook his head. "No, the next place. I'm thinking about New Orleans. Great city. Great tourist trap. I think we could do some good business there this winter."

"No, thanks," said Kai.

"I'm talking about real money," his father said.

"You're talking about another scam," Kai said. "I told you that's not my life anymore."

The Alien Frog Beast stiffened. "Oh, yeah, you're a hotshot surfer now. You're too good for that."

"Look, I don't want to remind you how many times you told me that you never wanted me in the first place," Kai said. "Truth is, I didn't exactly want you, either. But we got thrown together and you helped me out and I helped you out. I don't want to argue over who got a better deal, okay? And I also don't want to call up the credit card company and tell them how you run ten blanks off every foreign card that comes into this place. Because I have a feeling that might really put a dent in your profits. So just let me have the sketches, and then I'll get out of here and you'll never have to worry about feeding me or putting a roof over my head again."

Pat jerked his thumb toward the back room. "Your sketches are probably in there. Take 'em and get lost. You're right. I never wanted you in the first place and as far as I'm concerned, I hope I never see you again."

Kai went into the back. His half brother, Sean, was hunched over the computer, playing a game. He looked up at Kai and blinked in astonishment. "Hey!"

"How're you doing?" Kai clasped his hand.

"I don't know. Okay, I guess. How about you?"

"Getting by," Kai said.

"You come back?" There was a trace of hopefulness in the question.

"Just to get some sketches." The room looked like a garbage dump, the floor covered with candy wrappers and empty take-out bags, the other flat surfaces piled with unused transfers, odd unsold garments, box cutters, and tape. Kai went over to the desk and started to go through the piles of unopened letters and unpaid bills. The sketches had to be around there somewhere.

Sean's shoulders slumped. "You're not staying?"

"Sorry, dude."

Kai's half brother made a face and leaned close to him. "You sure you don't want to change your mind? He's been such a bastard since you left. I mean, he's *always* been a bastard, but it's gotten way worse. Yells at me all the time. Always telling me I'm useless. I can't stand it anymore."

"You want to come with me?" Kai asked.

Sean's eyes widened with surprise and uncertainty. "Where?"

"I don't know," Kai said. "Maybe we'll just stay here. We could find a cheap place to live and get jobs."

Sean's forehead bunched up. "Gee, I don't know. Just you and me by ourselves?"

"Sean, seriously, how old are you?"

"Uh, twenty-two."

"Isn't it time?" Kai asked. "I mean, you don't have to take his crap anymore."

Sean bit his lip. "I don't know."

"Think about it, okay?" Kai kept searching until he found the sketches under a pile of transfers.

"So that's it?" Sean asked. "You're just gonna go?"

"Like I said, you're welcome to come with me," Kai said. "I know some nice people in town. I think we'd be okay."

Sean looked at the door that led to the front of the store, then back at Kai. "I . . . I don't know."

"You don't have to decide now," Kai said. "If you go down to the beach there's a jetty. A lot of people surf there. If I'm not there, just ask around. Someone'll know where to find me."

Sean nodded mutely. Kai felt bad. His half brother wasn't evil like the Alien Frog Beast. He was just a guy who'd been beaten down so badly that he no longer knew who he was or what he was capable of. Kai patted him on the shoulder. "Think about it, Sean. I think we could be okay. I really do."

Twenty-six

"You're kidding me," Bean grumbled. "I mean, you've *really* got to be joking."

It was just after sunset, and they were sitting in the hearse on the street outside Tuck's Hardware. In the back of the hearse were six of the boards they'd taken back from Goldilocks.

"Bean, do you realize you've been saying that ever since I met you?" Kai said. "I mean, by now you've got to know the answer."

"Yeah." Bean nodded. "I guess I *know* the answer. It's *believing* the answer that I'm having a hard time with."

"This is not a big deal," Kai said. "All we have to do is take the boards up to Jade's apartment."

"Oh, is that all?" Bean asked sarcastically.

"You don't have to stick around for the rest of it," Kai said.

"Know what?" Bean said. "For once I'm going to take you up on that. As soon as we get these boards upstairs, I'm out of here."

"No problem," Kai said. He hesitated, then added. "There is just one other thing."

"I knew it!" Bean shook his head wearily.

"When we're done, we're gonna have to bring the boards back down."

"And?" Bean said suspiciously.

"Get the other ones and bring 'em back to Curtis."

"And?" Bean said.

"That's all," Kai said.

"Swear?" Bean asked.

"Swear," said Kai.

One by one they carried the boards up the dimly lit stairs and into Jade's apartment.

"Why are we putting them in the bedroom?" Bean asked.

"It'll add to the element of surprise," Kai answered.

"I bet," Bean said. "You know, I'm starting to think you enjoy stuff like this. I mean, bringing bad guys to justice and all that."

"Maybe I'm making up for past sins," Kai said.

"Oh, yeah?" Bean perked up. "Tell me. I'm all ears."

"Another time, okay?" Kai said.

"Where is Jade, anyway?" Bean asked when they'd finished getting the boards into the bedroom.

"She's preparing the turkey for the oven," Kai said.

"You just better hope that turkey doesn't explode," Bean said. "I'd hate to see you with gravy all over your face. No, forget that. What I'd really hate is to find you on my cadaver table in the embalming room tomorrow morning."

"Time will tell," Kai said. "But either way, thanks for the help."

No sooner did Bean leave than Everett arrived with his camcorder.

"Thanks for coming, dude," Kai said.

"No sweat," said the dreadlocked black kid. "There is nothing lower than a surfboard thief, and nothing I'd like more than to help nail one."

Kai led him into Jade's bedroom. Everett grinned when he saw Curtis's long boards spread out and propped up against the walls.

"This is funny. So where do you want the camera?"

"Someplace where he won't see it," said Kai. "We just need to get a clear shot of him in the doorway with good sound. You sure there's gonna be enough light?"

"No problem as long as we keep the lights on." Everett looked around the room and pointed at a tall bureau in the corner. On top of the bureau was a collection of plastic and metallic lipstick tubes and makeup kits. "I'll put it there and duck behind the bureau."

Everett had just finished setting up the digital camcorder when Kai heard the door open downstairs. "It's them," he said.

Kai left the bedroom door open about an inch so he could hear what was happening in the other room. Everett crouched down behind the bureau. Kai reclined in a chair. He heard the front door to the apartment open.

"Hey, nice place," said Dave McAllister, the chairman of Sun Haven Surf's board room. His words sounded sloppy. Kai had suggested to Jade that she encourage him to have a few drinks before they came back to her place.

"Thanks," said Jade. "So, can I get you something?"

"You know what I want," Big Dave said.

Real smooth, Kai thought with a silent groan. He was going to owe Jade big-time after this.

"Okay, okay," Jade said. Kai could picture her trying to fight him off. "Not here. Let's go into the bedroom."

"Yeah!" Big Dave practically shouted with glee.

The bedroom door swung open. Jade came in and immediately stepped to the side, so that her visitor would have a clear view of Kai in the chair. A split second later Dave appeared in the doorway. When he saw Kai and the surfboards his mouth fell open, and his eyes practically popped out of his head. Kai sure hoped Everett was getting all this on the camcorder.

"Hey, Dave, how're you doing?" Kai asked with a friendly smile.

"Wha—What is this? What are these boards doing here?" Dave sputtered. His eyes fell on Kai. "What the hell are *you* doing here?"

"Recognize these boards?" Kai asked.

"I . . . uh . . . . No, never saw them before in my life."

"That's not what Albert Hines says," Kai said. "He says you broke into Curtis Ames's shed and stole these boards and then sold them all to him."

Big Dave turned pale. "He told you that?"

"Come on, Dave," Kai said. "How else could I have gotten the boards?"

"Oh, shit." Dave turned pale.

"Personally, I don't get it," Kai said. "You don't seem like the kind of guy who goes around stealing another man's quiver."

"I—I didn't want to," Dave stammered, his shoulders sloping down. "Buzzy made me."

"Buzzy?" Kai pretended to be surprised. "Why would Buzzy do that?"

"To fuck with Curtis's head because he wants the old guy out of here something fierce," Dave said. "He said I should just get rid of them, but I couldn't do it."

"'Cause you wanted the money," Kai said.

"No, man, I just couldn't destroy these boards. They're too fricken beautiful. I mean, I sold them to Albert for a song. I didn't even want the money. I just couldn't trash 'em, and I didn't know what else to do." Dave looked like he was going to cry. "Aw, crap, man, what am I gonna do now? If Buzzy finds out I didn't get rid of these boards he's gonna can my sorry ass."

"I don't think so," Kai said.

Dave raised his head, surprised. "Why not?"

"Because it was Buzzy who told you to break into Curtis's shed and take them in the first place, right?"

"Yeah. So what?"

"So if Buzzy gives you any trouble, you can tell everyone it was his idea," Kai said.

"Oh, sure, like they'd believe me," Dave scoffed. "Fricken Buzzy Frank is Mr. Sun Haven himself. No one's gonna believe me over him. Not in a million years."

"You might be surprised."

Dave seemed to get hold of himself. His eyebrows dropped. "How'd you say you got these boards?"

"I said I got them from Albert," Kai said.

Dave frowned. "You bought 'em? All of them?"

"Not exactly," Kai said. "But I don't think he's gonna want them back now. The boards go back to Curtis where they belong."

Dave looked at Jade. "This is why you invited me here?"

"Sorry."

"The hell you are," Dave sniffed.

"Hey, be nice," Kai said. "In fact, you should be thankful. Now Curtis is going to get his boards back, and you won't have to go through the rest of your life feeling guilty about taking another man's quiver."

"Dude, you got a strange way of turning things around," Dave said.

"Funny you should mention turning around," said Kai. "Because that's exactly what I think you should do. Just turn around and leave. Don't tell anyone what happened here and you'll probably be okay."

Dave's eyes darted back and forth between Kai and Jade. "You gonna tell Curtis I'm the one who took his boards? Or the cops?"

"I don't see why I'd have to," Kai said. "Not if you just go along and pretend like this never happened."

"Then it's not me you're really interested in, is it?" Dave said.

"Very good," said Kai.

"Okay, I won't say a word," Dave said. He started to turn in the doorway, then stopped and looked at Jade one last time. Kai could see Jade brace herself for something nasty. But

Dave only shook his head, a bit sadly, Kai thought, then turned and left.

Jade followed him to the front door and locked it, then came back to the bedroom. By now Everett had slipped out from behind the bureau.

"I thought that went pretty well," Jade said. "Did you get what you wanted?"

"I sure hope so," Kai said, and looked at Everett. "Did you get it all on the camcorder?"

"It's in the can," Everett answered with a wink.

Twenty-seven

From Jade's apartment Kai called Bean to come back and help him take the boards over to the Driftwood Motel. On Seaside Drive, it seemed like almost every third car was carrying a quiver of boards for the next day's event.

"I've never seen anything like this," Bean said. "I mean, this is big-time."

They got to the motel. The no vacancy sign was on.

"Got a full house?" Kai asked when Curtis came out of the office to help them move the boards into his apartment.

"Bursting at the seams," Curtis said. "This just might be the biggest surfing event to ever hit Sun Haven."

They put all the boards in Curtis's living room.

"I don't know how I can pay you back for this, grom," the older man said, walking with Kai and Bean back out to the hearse. By now it was after ten. The town was starting to quiet down and there was a slight coolness in the air.

"Believe me, old man, you've already paid me back," Kai said. "Any news about the tax situation?"

Curtis shrugged. "Could hear something any day now. Only it ain't a question of whether or not I can keep the motel. It's just a question of how long until I have to sell it."

"Sorry to hear that," Kai said.

"Me too," said Curtis. "But it don't mean we can't continue to fight the good fight, grom."

"What do you mean?" Kai asked.

"Just what I said. They may win a battle here and there, but the war is far from over," Curtis said, then changed the subject. "So, tomorrow's the big day. Weather and waves should be pretty good. Any thoughts?"

"I actually haven't had time to think about it," Kai answered.

"Well, grom, as a great man once said,

'Whatever gets you through the night.' Know what I mean?"

"I guess."

Curtis held out his hand and shook Bean's and Kai's. "Again, boys, thanks. Getting those boards back is something I never expected. It kind of gives a fellow hope."

Bean and Kai got into the hearse. Bean drove back onto Main Street. It was late and the street was empty.

"I, for one, am going to bed," Bean said. "I'll need a good night's sleep if I'm gonna give the long board competition a shot tomorrow. You feel like powering down?"

"Think I'll go down to the beach for a while," Kai said.

Bean pulled into the parking lot. Brightly painted vans from Billabong, Hurley, Quiksilver, and Volcom were parked near the boardwalk.

"Looks like the gang's all here," Bean said, braking the hearse to a stop.

"Thanks for everything, dude," Kai said. "Catch you in the morning." He got out of the car and crossed the boardwalk. Directly in front of Screamers stood a large white tent with open sides as well as smaller tents emblazoned with the names of various surf gear manufacturers. A line of light blue Porta Pottis stood behind the main tent. Kai walked toward the water. It was a dark, moonless night and there were more clouds than stars in the sky. A cool, damp breeze was coming out of the south. Here and there on the sand couples huddled in the dark. About a quarter of a mile down the beach, a bunch of flashlight beams swung this way and that, and Kai suspected that a bunch of kids staying at one of the beach resorts had gotten permission from their parents to stay out late.

Kai sat down on the dry side of the tide mark and gazed at the inky waves crashing into ghostly white foam. In the absence of the moon, and with clouds covering a lot of the stars, the water was as dark and ominous as Kai had ever seen it. He thought about the past few months here in Sun Haven. Difficult months, but still the best since he'd left Hawaii.

After a while the flashlights headed up the beach. The couples who were within sight also got up and left, leaving Kai alone with the mild crash of the waves, the drifting dark clouds, and a lone seagull that now and then swooped out of the dark.

"Hi," someone said behind him.

Kai turned and saw Shauna, dressed in jeans and a sweatshirt.

"Busy?" she asked.

"Very," Kai said. "Think you could come back tomorrow?"

Shauna hesitated, as if she couldn't tell whether he was serious.

"Hey, come on." Kai patted the sand beside him.

She sat down. For a while they stared at the ocean and didn't say anything.

"Bean told you I was here?" Kai finally asked.

"Uh-huh. Come down here to think?"

"Hmm."

More silence followed, then Shauna asked, "What are you thinking about?"

"Not much."

"Not about tomorrow?"

"Not really," Kai said.

"You know, if you enter and win first or second prize, you could pay Bean back for the tires," Shauna said.

Kai turned to look at her. "He didn't send you down here to tell me that, did he?"

Shauna shook her head. "He never even told me what happened. I found out from Booger."

"Okay."

"I just feel bad for him," Shauna said.

"Me too," said Kai.

"Kai, just because you enter a competition, it won't make you a jerk," Shauna said. "You are who you are. Being in a competition doesn't change you into someone you're not."

Kai gazed at the dark waves. He knew she was right, but it was more complicated than that. Way more complicated.

"Kai?" Shauna said more softly.

"Hmmm?"

"What happened in Kauai?"

The question settled on his shoulders like a weight. "I told you. I was a hypercompetitive jerk. The worst kind of local. I thought I was the hottest thing on a board."

"But what *happened*?"

Overhead, between the drifting clouds, a patch of twinkling stars appeared. Kai took a deep breath and felt a quivering sensation inside. He had never told anyone, but maybe it was time. "Being a hypercompetitive local jerk isn't the same on Kauai as it is here. There's not just one break that everyone wants to surf. There's a series of breaks, each one a little more gnarly than the last. So at the same time that you're being a dickhead and keeping kooks off your break, the guys on the next break are doing the same thing to you."

"So you have to work your way up?" Shauna guessed.

"Yeah, and for it to really mean something, you have to do it when the surf is big and dangerous. Like on a day when even the locals think it's too wicked to go out. The idea is you go out on a day like that and show them what you can do, and they're supposed to be so in awe that they feel honored to let you into the lineup."

"So that day came, right?"

Kai nodded. He scooped up a handful of sand and let the grains tumble between his fingers. "Yeah, it was the kind of day when they couldn't waste the energy keeping you off the break because it was so big and hairy that everyone was too busy fighting for their own survival. A lot of people told me not to go out, but to me that just meant it was my shot."

"So you went," Shauna said.

"Of course. Only it was probably twice as big as anything I'd ever been in before and I was scared shitless," Kai said. "But I'd read all the stories about how the big-wave guys get scared, and how the whole thing is about facing your fear and overcoming it. So even though every ounce of my soul was telling me I was way over my head, I just went for it."

Shauna waited silently. The dark waves crashed. A crab skittered along the water's edge.

"I got outside and was totally freaked," Kai continued. "I mean, I'd never seen waves like these before. They were so damn big and coming so damn fast that you couldn't catch them even when you tried. They'd lift you up and drop you down like you were on a Ferris wheel or something. I'd see a wave coming and I'd start to paddle like crazy, and the wave would pull the water up the face under me so fast that I was actually going backward. And the next thing I'd know, the wave would pull me right back over itself and leave me behind."

"Until . . ."

"I had to totally commit," Kai said. "I got myself under a peak where I was so deep in the curl that I was either gonna catch the wave or get creamed. There was no escape. I was in that wave one way or the other, for better or worse."

"And?"

"I went over the falls."

"What's that mean?" Shauna asked.

"I got caught in the crest of the wave as it curled over and dropped. When that happens, you get lifted up and then driven down into the trough with a few tons of water slamming down on top of you. And the trough, of course, is the shallowest part of the wave."

Shauna winced. "You hit bottom?"

"Yeah, only it wasn't sand like it is here," Kai said. "It was reef. And you don't just hit it. You bounce off it over and over and it tears you to shreds."

Shauna touched the scar on Kai's knee.

"Right," Kai said. "Took the skin off like sandpaper. Also broke my collarbone and put a gash in my head that took a hundred and sixty-three stitches to close."

"I guess I can see how that might change your attitude," said Shauna.

Kai felt a bitter smile on his lips. "You want to know the truth? If that had been all the damage, it probably wouldn't have changed anything. I probably would have been back out there being as big a jerk as ever, as soon as I was healthy again."

"Then what did happen?" Shauna asked.

"I got trashed in the water for a while, and then they got me out and put me in a car and took me to the hospital," Kai said. "And . . ." He trailed off. It was too difficult to continue.

"And?" Shauna prompted him softly.

"Someone called my mom."

Shauna was quiet. Kai suspected she was slowly putting together all the bits and pieces he'd revealed over the past few months. He could feel the dread building up in him as the inevitable happened and she finally figured it out.

"Oh, God," she whispered. "The narrow bridge."

Kai felt as if someone had stuck a knife into his very core.

"Then it wasn't the other driver's fault?" she asked gently.

Kai shook his head. Up above, the clouds closed over the patch of starlit sky. "It was my fault."

"No, Kai."

"Come on, Shauna," he said. "There's no way she would have raced over that bridge if it hadn't been for me."

"What happened to the other driver?"

"Hardly a scratch," Kai said. "He was driving a big SUV with air bags."

"And your mom?"

"A rusty old pickup. And she never wore her seat belt."

They listened to the waves. Kai could feel his thoughts and memories stretching all the way back to Hawaii, just like the dark water before him stretched down the eastern coasts of North and South America, around Cape Horn, out into the Pacific, and eventually to those very islands.

"Kai, you can't blame yourself."

"Give me one reason why not?"

"Because she could have waited for the other guy to go over the bridge. She could have worn her seat belt."

"If you heard that your son was badly hurt and in the hospital, would you have waited for the other guy?" Kai asked.

"Yes," Shauna said.

Kai didn't say what he was thinking—that she'd never had a kid and couldn't know what it felt like.

"Does this mean that for the last two years you've been carrying around this idea that it was your fault your mom died?" Shauna asked.

"And that if you hadn't been such a hot dog, and so competitive about getting into the next biggest break, this never would have happened?"

Kai didn't answer.

"So you don't want to surf in the Northeast Championship because if you do, you're afraid you'll turn back into that other Kai? The hypercompetitive local who got his mom killed?"

Kai placed his hands flat on the sand and began to push himself up. He felt her hand on his shoulder, stopping him.

"Don't," she said.

Kai froze, then slowly lowered himself back to the sand again.

"It's not going to happen, Kai," Shauna said.

"How do you know?" Kai asked.

"Did you think that if you entered the contest tomorrow you'd forget? You can't. You're a different person than you were two years ago. No matter what you do now, you could never go back to being that person again."

Kai looked at her. "You sure?"

"Yes, Kai, I'm sure."

Twenty-eight

As soon as the first hint of light appeared the next morning, a steady parade of vehicles began to arrive at the parking lot. Bean managed to get one of the last spots. By the time the sun came up, vehicles loaded with boards and surfers were dropping gear and bodies off, then driving away to park elsewhere. The beach was filling up with competitors and their families.

Kai and Bean carried their boards toward the boardwalk where Everett was waiting for them on a bench. He was wearing a small green day pack.

Kai clasped his hand. "Thanks for coming."

"No problem." Everett reached into the

day pack and pulled out the camcorder. "Try not to drop it in the sand, okay?"

"You got it."

Everett closed the pack. "I'm gonna get lost in the crowd. Catch you later."

He went down the beach. A line of last-minute entrants was forming outside the big white tent. Manufacturers' reps were starting to open the smaller tents and getting ready to display their products. The shoulder-high sets out at Screamers were almost wall to wall with surfers eager to get a ride in before the competition actually began.

"You gonna wait here?" Bean asked Kai.

"Yeah."

"Give me your board." Bean held out his free arm so Kai could slide his board under it. "I'll take it down to the beach."

"Thanks," Kai said.

"Good luck," Bean said. "You'll need it."

It wasn't long before the yellow Hummer pulled into the parking lot. Lucas and Buzzy got out with a thick board bag. Kai guessed there were three boards inside. Buzzy got back in the Hummer and drove away to find a parking space while Lucas came across the boardwalk.

Kai stepped into his path. Lucas stopped.

"So you're here to compete?" he asked.

"Maybe," Kai said.

Lucas scowled. "Why aren't you on the beach?"

"I want to show you something." Kai opened the camcorder screen and pressed play. It was the scene in Jade's bedroom with Dave McAllister admitting that Buzzy ordered him to steal Curtis's boards.

Lucas put down the board bag and watched silently. The video ended and he looked at Kai. "That for real?"

"You think Dave could ever act that well if it wasn't?" Kai asked back.

Lucas neither moved nor spoke. Then a sneer appeared on his lips. "Yeah, so? What's your point?"

"I just thought you should know," said Kai.

"Everybody knows my old man wants Curtis out," Lucas said. "That's not news."

"You think it was right for him to tell Dave to steal Curtis's boards?" Kai asked.

"He does what he has to do to win," Lucas said.

"Including break the law?"

"Look who's talking," Lucas said. "Your old man's a crook from way back."

"Right, and I walked away," Kai said. "What are *you* gonna do?"

"Fuck you," Lucas said. He picked up the board bag and headed for the beach.

Kai was closing Everett's camcorder when Curtis and Shauna came out of the crowd now flooding across the boardwalk toward the beach. The competition would begin soon. Shauna gestured to the camera. "You showed it to Lucas?"

"Yeah."

"What'd he say?"

"Nothing friendly."

"Not what you hoped, huh?" said Curtis.

Kai shook his head. He was disappointed. "Maybe it was just a stupid fantasy."

"You know what they say," Curtis said. "Like father, like son."

Not in my case, Kai thought. *But maybe in most others.*

By now the line at the sign-up tent had grown long. The contest director was addressing a big crowd of competitors with the usual warnings about dropping in, snaking, and interferences.

"There's still time to sign up," Shauna said. Kai didn't respond.

"You can do it," Shauna urged him. "No matter what happens, I promise you'll still be you. You're not going to forget everything that's happened. You'll never go back to the person you were before."

Kai looked at Curtis questioningly.

"Listen, grom, if there was no contest today, would you be out there surfing?" the older man asked.

Kai looked out at the waves. The sets were coming in evenly. Shoulder high, breaking cleanly. Who wouldn't go surfing on a day like this? "Yeah, I imagine I would."

"So you just gonna let some stupid Northeast Championship stop you?"

Kai grinned. "When you look at it that way, why should I?"

Curtis rubbed Kai's head. "That's the spirit."

Twenty-nine

The tense mist of competition was thick in the air. This wasn't some small, local, "let's all go out and have fun" kind of event. No one smiled or joked. When Kai looked around, he saw nothing but grim determination on the faces of his fellow competitors. And there were plenty of good surfers out there. People who could rip and work a wave until there was nothing left but soup. Kai surfed with total resolve, concentration, and intensity. Tomorrow he could go back to being a soul surfer.

It was a long day, and by midafternoon everyone from Sun Haven except Kai, Lucas, and Bean had been eliminated. Bean was in the men's long board finals when Booger, Spazzy, and Jillian showed up.

"Hey, guys!" Spazzy twitched as he wound his way through the patchwork of blankets, beach towels, and umbrellas. Booger and Jillian followed. Kai could see from the way Jillian kept swiveling her head that she was looking for Bean.

"He's out there." Kai pointed out at the break, where six long boarders in colored jerseys were jockeying for waves.

"How's he doing?" Booger asked.

"Hard to tell," Kai said. "They're all good. At this point it probably has as much to do with luck as anything else."

An air horn blared twice. Bean's heat was over. A few minutes later he trudged up the beach with his board under his arm and seawater dripping off the end of his long braided ponytail. His head was down and it was hard to tell whether he was bummed or just tired. But when he saw Jillian, he straightened up and smiled.

"How come you're not over at the tent waiting for the results?" Booger asked.

"They don't announce the winners until the awards ceremony," Bean said, sounding dejected. "But I didn't get enough good rides. It's unbelievable out there. You can hardly get on a wave. Every time you think you're ready to go, there's some other dude already paddling into it."

"You mean they're snaking you?" Booger asked.

"Maybe, but it's hard to tell," Bean said. "These guys just know where to be. No matter how deep in the pocket you think you are, there's always someone a little deeper."

Jillian put her hand on Bean's shoulder.

"This the way it was in the old days?" Kai asked Curtis.

The older man shook his head. "The competition's fiercer, the stakes are bigger. These guys are in top shape. Look at 'em. Their shoulders, and arms, and legs. You can see they train like athletes. Back in my day, we competed hard, but there was a feeling that you still let everyone have his shot. That's not here anymore. You don't get your shot unless you fight for it. That fight starts in a gym, lifting weights, and on a track, doing endurance work. When I was on the circuit, the only things we lifted were boards and beer bottles. There are boys out there today doing things world champions weren't doing when I competed."

"Well, sure," Bean teased. "Back in those days it wasn't easy to catch air on a hundred-and-eighty-pound, fifteen-foot solid-redwood board."

"Screw you," Curtis growled in a good-natured way. "By the end of my time on the tour they were starting to use short boards. The forerunners of what you kids are on today."

"Men's open finals," the beach marshal announced through the megaphone. "Competitors get your jerseys."

Kai rose to his feet and picked up his board. His friends wished him good luck.

"You can do it, Kai."

"Give it your best shot, dude."

Kai was given a red jersey. He was one of six surfers in the men's final. Four were from out of town. He'd never seen them before. The sixth was Lucas, in a yellow jersey.

"Gather round, boys," the beach marshal said, and waited until the competitors came close. "Okay, you've already heard everything there is to know. Just one last thing. Be real careful about snaking one another's waves out there. There's been too much of that already today, and the judges are going to be watching closely. Wave selection's important, but remember everyone deserves a shot. You boys have worked hard to get to the finals today. You don't want to get eliminated for stealing someone else's wave. Any questions?"

No one said a word.

"All right then," the beach marshal said. "Anyone need to use a Porta Potti, this is your chance."

Kai decided to take advantage of the offer. The last thing he wanted to be thinking about out there was relieving himself. He went up the beach and behind the white tent.

When he came out of the Porta Potti, Buzzy Frank was waiting for him.

Thirty

"**G**ot a second?" Lucas's father asked.

"About that," Kai answered.

"I wanted to say that you've done exactly what I asked you to do," Buzzy said. "I doubt Lucas would have made it to the finals today if you hadn't pushed him these last few weeks."

Kai nodded silently and glanced at the crowd on the beach. Almost everyone was facing out toward the water, watching the surfers.

"But maybe you've pushed him far enough," Buzzy said.

Kai turned and looked at him. "What do you mean?"

"Everyone knows you don't care that

much about competing," Buzzy said. "In a way, if you win today, it's almost a waste, because you probably won't do anything with it."

"You want me to let Lucas win because you think he'll do more with it than I will?" Kai cut to the chase.

"Why not?" Buzzy said. "You've done it before. You let that Spazzy kid get into the finals at Fairport last month."

"Maybe I did that because I knew how much it would mean to him," Kai said.

"This would mean a lot to Lucas," Buzzy said.

"Maybe even more to you," said Kai.

"Maybe a lot for both of us," Buzzy said.

"And suppose I do back off," Kai said. "How's that gonna help Lucas at the next competition? You think the other surfers are gonna back off just because you ask them?"

"If Lucas gets a big win here I think he'll gain the confidence he needs to compete against the big boys. You know this isn't only about skill. It's about having the confidence to take risks. Lucas needs this win, Kai. This could be the beginning of something big for him."

"You're sure it's not the beginning of

something big for you?" Kai asked.

Buzzy narrowed his eyes. "Enough bullshit. I'll make this easy for you. The prize money's a thousand bucks. I'll double it."

Kai stared into Buzzy's eyes. "You know, I was over at the hospital the other day. I saw your name on that plaque for the new wing."

"What's that got to do with this?"

"That was a really good thing you did," Kai said.

Buzzy blinked, as if the compliment caught him off guard. "Why, thank you."

"It meant something to me," Kai said. "It meant you're not such a bad guy."

"Hey!" someone yelled. Kai turned and saw Lucas wave. "The heat's starting."

Kai looked back at Buzzy.

"I'm offering you two thousand bucks," Lucas's father said.

"Keep it," Kai said.

"Why?"

"Because you can't win everything every time." Kai turned and trotted back to the waiting area.

When he got there Lucas asked, "What was that about?"

"Ask him after the heat," Kai replied.

They grabbed their boards and headed for the water.

For the next twenty minutes Kai surfed pure death or glory. He was only vaguely aware of the other surfers. One in particular, in the light blue jersey, seemed to have a knack for catching the best waves. Almost every time the kid took off on a wave, Kai would hear cheers from the crowd on the beach.

The heat ended. Kai carried his board up the beach and was surprised to find only Bean waiting for him. He was a little disappointed that Curtis wasn't there.

"Looked pretty good out there, dude," Bean said.

"The kid in light blue looked better," Kai said.

"He was definitely amped," Bean allowed.

"So where is everyone?" Kai asked.

"Oh, you know, they had to make up something for Spazzy to do while Jillian put the finishing touches on the surprise party tonight," Bean said. "Come on. It's time for the awards."

They joined the crowd of competitors and onlookers in front of the white tent. Kai noticed that neither Lucas nor Buzzy was there. He spotted them down the beach, out of earshot. While Kai couldn't hear what they were saying, it was clear from their body language that it wasn't exactly a love fest.

"Wonder what that's about," Bean said.

"I think I know," Kai said.

"Buzzy's pissed at Lucas for not doing better?" Bean guessed.

"I'd bet it's the other way around," Kai said.

Bean frowned. The awards ceremony began with the contest director thanking the manufacturers and sponsors who helped organize and finance the event. Then the trophies and checks were given out to the winners and runners-up in each event. As usual the biggest and most important contest, the men's short board, was announced last. By then most of the crowd had gone.

The contest director held up a large gold trophy. "First prize in the men's short board division goes to Mark Wickersham of Belmar."

Cheers broke out of the crowd, and the kid who'd been wearing the light blue jersey bounded up to the front to accept his trophy and check for $1,000. Cameras clicked as he held up the trophy. Moments later, as he left the awards area, the writers and photographers from the magazines converged on him.

Next the contest director held up a smaller gold trophy. "Second prize goes to Kai Herter of Sun Haven."

Bean hooted and whistled. There was a smattering of applause when Kai accepted the trophy and check for $500. No cameras clicked. No writers surrounded him. In surfing, as in life, there was a big difference between winner and runner-up.

Bean and Kai headed over to the hearse and slid their boards in the back, then got in the front. Kai took a ballpoint pen from behind the sun visor. He turned his check for second place over and wrote, "Pay to Lawrence Balter" on the back, then signed his name.

"Here you go, dude." He handed the check to Bean.

Bean scowled, then nodded as if he understood. "The tires?"

"What else?" Kai said.

They were driving back through town when Kai thought of something.

"Hey, Bean, could you go up East Street?"

Bean turned the hearse at the corner. "What's up?"

"There's something I need to see," Kai said. "Shouldn't take long."

They drove up the block and stopped in front of T-licious. A heavy, balding man in a rumpled gray suit was taping a white sheet of paper to the glass front door.

"Uh-oh," Bean said. "That looks serious."

Kai got out of the hearse and stepped onto the sidewalk. The early evening breeze made the leaves on the trees reveal their dull silvery undersides. The air felt light and dry today. Now that it was early evening, the sunlight had a different, clearer slant than before.

The man's round face was red. Beads of sweat dotted his forehead. The white sheet of paper said, in big letters, CLOSED BY ORDER OF FOURTH CIRCUIT COURT. Beneath that were several official-looking paragraphs of smaller print. At the bottom were signatures. One by a judge. The other by the county sheriff.

"What's it mean?" Kai asked the man.

"This place has been shut down by order of the county," the fat man said.

"Why?"

"Guy who ran it is in all kinds of trouble. He got caught selling counterfeit knockoffs of name-brand clothing. And it turns out he's wanted in other states for mail fraud, tax evasion, and credit card theft. I'm glad I'm not in his shoes."

"Know where he is right now?" Kai asked.

"County lockup. And from what I hear, he's gonna be there for a long time."

Kai walked back to the hearse and got in.

"What'd he say?" Bean asked.

"Looks like my father stuck around too long," Kai said.

"So where is he?"

"Someplace where he can't just pack up and leave," Kai said.

Bean pulled the hearse from the curb. "We better get back to my place and wash up. We're supposed to be at Spazzy's in half an hour."

"He still doesn't know it's a surprise?" Kai asked.

"I dropped a couple of hints at the beach before and he didn't react to any of them," Bean said. "I think he's gonna be blown away."

Kai smiled. "Good."

"You get a sense of whether Lucas and his crew are going to show?" Bean asked.

"Hard to say," Kai said. "Lucas sure didn't look happy there at the end."

"Yeah, guess you're right," Bean said.

Back at Bean's place they showered and changed clothes. They got back into the hearse and drove to Spazzy's. The only car parked in the driveway was the black Mercedes station wagon with the California plates. Kai felt a little uncomfortable. Either Jillian and Deb Hollister had done a really good job of hiding cars where Spazzy wouldn't see them, or it was going to be a very poorly attended surprise party.

"So where is Spazzy supposed to be anyway?" Kai asked.

"I don't know," Bean said. "Shauna and Booger said they'd take care of that."

Bean parked the hearse out of sight around the corner, and Kai and he walked back to Spazzy's house and up the path to the front door. Bean rapped his knuckles against the door.

It seemed odd to Kai that he didn't press the doorbell.

The front door opened, and Kai found himself looking at a sea of smiling faces in the doorway. "Surprise!" they all shouted.

Naturally Kai turned and looked back down the path, assuming that Spazzy was coming up behind them. But the path was empty. Kai turned and looked again at the faces in the doorway. Spazzy was one of them. What was he doing there if it was a surprise party for him? It didn't make sense. Then he noticed that Bean was also smiling at him.

"Surprise, Kai," he said.

Son of a bitch!

Thirty-one

Kai had been eight years old the last time someone threw a surprise party for him. His mom and Ethan said that for his birthday they were taking him to Zelo's Beach House, a restaurant that was not on the beach, but was a cool grown-up place to go. When they got there, Kai discovered seven of his closest friends already sitting at a big table. They ate burgers and fries, and drank way too much soda. The cake, of course, was shaped like a surfboard.

Now Kai stood on the walk outside Spazzy's front door, trying to figure out why they were throwing a party for him. Shauna came out of the house, slipped her arm through his, and led him inside. The crowd at the doorway parted to let them in. Only Spazzy remained in front of them, twitching. He licked the palm of his hand, sniffed it, then held it out to Kai, who understandably hesitated for a second, then shook it. The others gathered around them in the living room. In addition to Kai's friends and Jillian, Kai spotted Jade, Everett, Curtis, and Teddy (nowhere near Curtis). Besides Everett, no one in Lucas's crew had shown up.

Spazzy took a wrinkled piece of paper out of his pocket and unfolded it. Kai realized it was some kind of speech.

"I wrote this for you," Spazzy said, and began to read: "Dear Kai, Knowing you, you're probably wondering why we're having this party. Well, the reason is that everyone in this room feels that this summer you helped us become better people. You either taught us something important, or made the summer more fun for us, or did something that made us look at life differently. We know it'll probably embarrass you if we start telling you all the good stuff you did, so we won't. Besides, if you think about it, it'll probably be pretty obvious anyway. So we got together and decided to give you this party for two reasons. The first is to let you know that we appreciate everything you did this summer. The second reason is to say that we all hope you'll find a way to stay in Sun Haven. Because we really want you to." Spazzy started to fold up the piece of paper. "That's it, dude. Short speech. I hope it wasn't too cheesy."

"Well." Kai grinned. "It was pretty cheesy. But I appreciate it just the same. Thanks, Spazzy."

Everyone clapped. As the clapping died down, a short, awkward silence followed. "Okay, guys," Spazzy said, "the touchy-feely part of the party is over. Time to go out to the pool and have fun."

Everyone went out the sliding doors to the back. Those who wanted to swim went into the cabana and changed into trucks and swimsuits. Those who didn't gathered around the food. Once again Jillian had hired the bald guy with the ponytail who'd cooked for them on the Fourth of July. This time he served barbequed ribs and chicken.

Kai found himself standing beside Teddy while they waited to fill their plates.

"I looked at those sketches," Teddy said. "They're not bad. I'd change the colors a bit."

"Then you're serious about opening your own shop?" Kai asked.

Teddy shook her head. "Not yet. But I figure I'll put up some signs around town and run ads in the local papers and see what happens. If I can get a business going that way, then maybe I'll think about opening a shop."

"Great," Kai said.

"But I'm afraid I'm going to need that thruster back that I gave you," she said.

That stung. Kai gazed down at the patio. He loved that board. Even if he hadn't finished paying Teddy back for it, he hated to give it up.

"Just temporarily," Teddy added, "until my assistant has time to sand it down and put my new logo on and re-glass it."

"Your assistant?" Kai repeated, confused.

"*You*, dummy."

Kai grinned.

"I wouldn't look so happy," Teddy warned him. "You'll be lucky to earn minimum wage."

"Maybe he won't need much more than that," Bean said, joining them. "After all, he could be living rent free."

Kai eyed him suspiciously. "How's that?"

"My roomie, dude." Bean put his arm

around Kai's shoulder. "And since I live rent free, so would you."

"What about mortuary college?" Kai asked.

"I'll be home on the weekends," Bean said. "I've kind of gotten used to having a live body around."

Kai didn't know what to say. Suddenly he had a job and a place to stay.

"Guys, I'm really touched," he said. "Truly. You'll understand if it takes a while for all of this to sink in, right?"

"Take your time," Bean said, and went off to speak to Jillian.

For the next few hours Kai partied with his friends. Later, in the dark, he walked down to the beach with Curtis. It was another moonless night, and the black sky was speckled with shimmering stars. They stood at the waterline.

"Think you'll stay?" the older man asked.

"Don't know," Kai answered. "Not sure I'd have anyplace else to go, even if I wanted to."

Out past the breaking waves half a dozen small white terns with black-capped heads and pointy wings dive-bombed the surface, often emerging with a wriggling silver-sided shiner in their black-tipped yellow beaks.

"What about you?" Kai asked.

"'Fraid it's time to close up shop, grom."

"You're selling the motel?"

"It's the only way I can pay off all those back taxes. But the truth is, I'm ready to go. I'm tried of the whole damn thing. Tired of getting grief from the damn town. Tired of being harassed. They want to get rid of the Driftwood that bad, let 'em."

"But then they're going to win," Kai said. "This place really will become Buzzy Land."

"Not quite," Curtis said. "See, there's this organization called the Shore and Beach Preservation Association, and it turns out that they don't want all this beach land being developed any more than you or me. They have special funds set aside to buy parcels of seashore when they become available. Problem is, they usually can't come up with the kind of money guys like Buzzy can. On the other hand they can make special allowances for the property that guys like Buzzy would never make."

"Like?"

"In return for an agreement to preserve the dunes and beach and land near the beach, they might be inclined to allow for a parking lot and picnic area up near the road. They might even be inclined to allow for the construction of a small shack to rent surfboards and other stuff people going to the beach might need."

"So it would be like a park?" Kai asked.

"Like a park run by a private nonprofit organization," Curtis said.

"But that still means surfers would have no place to stay around here," Kai said.

"Not right on the beach," Curtis said. "But after I pay those back taxes, I should still have enough left to be able to get a place back on the other side of town, where I could run a small rooming house. Like one of those bed-and-breakfast deals. I admit it wouldn't be within walking distance, but surfers could stay at my place and then drive down to the beach in the morning."

Kai and Curtis watched the terns feed on the shiners.

"I guess what I'm trying to say, grom, is you can't stop progress," Curtis finally said. "But if you're smart about it, you might be able to make progress take a detour."

They walked back up the beach. It was late by now, and people were starting to leave. Kai thanked them one by one, and told them he'd see them soon.

Then it was Jade's turn. They faced each other in the doorway.

"So, I guess I'll see you around," Kai said.

"Don't forget, you still owe me big-time," she said.

"I'll make it up to you," Kai said. "I promise."

Jade gave him an amused look. "I've heard that before."

"Let me know what I can do, okay?" Kai said.

Jade leaned forward and pressed herself against him. Placing her lips close to his ear, she whispered, "I think you can figure that out by yourself."

Kai felt her tongue brush his earlobe, and then she was walking away into the night.

Kai turned and found Shauna waiting in the hallway.

"I hope you plan to wash your ear," she said.

Kai smiled at her. But she surprised him by stepping close and kissing him hard on the lips. Then she backed away.

"I know you don't like competition," she said. "But I think some things are worth competing for."

"In this case I'd have to agree," Kai said.

"Good." Shauna kissed him again, then stepped past him and down the path that led from Spazzy's house.

Kai closed the front door.

Finally they'd all left except Bean, who was helping Jillian and Marta clean up.

Kai and Spazzy sat on some chairs next to the pool, gazing at the sparkling aqua-blue water lit by the underwater light.

"This was great, Spazzy," Kai said. "Thanks, dude."

"Were you really surprised?" Spazzy asked.

"Are you kidding?" Kai chuckled. "Totally."

They listened to the crickets chirp in the dark.

"You know, we're leaving for California tomorrow," Spazzy said.

"You and Jillian drive?" Kai asked.

"Yeah. Marta stays and closes up the house, then flies out. We plan it so we all get to Santa Barbara around the same time."

The wind chimes clinked.

"I'll be sorry to see you go," Kai said.

"I know you're not sure where you'll be next summer," Spazzy said, "but you'll stay in touch, won't you?"

"Absolutely," Kai said.

"Thanks, dude. I guess I don't have to tell you again that this has been the best summer of my life."

Kai smelled the salt scent of the breeze coming off the ocean. He heard the crash of the waves. He thought about the friends he'd made over the past few months.

"For me, too, Spazzy," Kai said. "For me, too."

Thirty-two

Jail smelled.

Otherwise it was pretty much like what you saw on TV. Bars and reinforced metal doors and superthick shatterproof glass. Surveillance cameras and guards in uniforms who tried to look relaxed, but were secretly alert and sized you up as if trying to decide how much chance there was that you might be smuggling in a weapon or drugs or something else the prisoners weren't supposed to have.

But the one thing TV didn't get across was the smell of body odor and chemical disinfectant. Both distinct and strong and entrenched, as if the war between them had been going on too long and had reached a stalemate.

"This way." A large blond woman in a uniform led Kai down a corridor. The gun, baton, radio, and can of mace hanging from her black police belt thudded against her hips as she walked, and Kai wondered if that annoyed her or was something one just got used to after a while.

They stopped at yet another reinforced metal door with a small glass window at eye level. The woman guard peered through the window, then pressed a button in the wall. The door slid open.

"In there," the woman said, in that tone of voice that indicated he was now being handed off to another guard.

Kai went through the doorway and found himself in a narrow room with a long table divided by low partitions at regular intervals and a chair at each station. A thick wall of scuffed Plexiglas ran down the center of the table, with large white numbers above each partition. There were holes in the Plexiglas to permit conversation between two people sitting across from each other.

"Name?" a guard inside the door said.

"Kai Herter."

The guard scanned a clipboard. "Number three."

Kai went down to number three. His father was sitting on the other side of the Plexiglas, wearing dark green coveralls. He looked exactly as he always did, unshaven, hair askew, his eyes appearing to bulge behind the thick square-framed glasses. Kai sat down in the chair.

"So what do you want?" the Alien Frog Beast asked.

The coldness of the remark caught Kai by surprise. "Good to see you, too," he shot back.

Pat rolled his eyes and started to get up. "I don't have time for this."

"From what I hear, you're going to have plenty of time," Kai said.

His father stopped, then sat down again. His shoulders slumped forward. Kai felt bad. The guy was a crook, but he was also his father. The only real family he had left.

"What's gonna happen to Sean?" Kai asked.

"I took the fall for him," his father said. "No sense in us both going away. He's got a sister outside of Chicago. She's from his mom's first marriage. She wants him to come out there."

"What's gonna happen to you?" Kai asked.

"I've got four states pressing charges plus all the federal counts against me. Guess they're gonna keep me here until they figure out how to divide me up."

"Any idea where you'll wind up?"

Pat shrugged. "My lawyer says the Feds usually win over the states in situations like this. So they'll have first crack at me. They'll probably want to send me to Ray Brook. My lawyer says he'll try to get me into Otisville."

"Prisons?" Kai asked.

"Yeah. Ray Brook's medium security. Like I'm dangerous, right?" His father snorted in disgust. "Otisville's minimum security."

"You could work in the prison store," Kai said.

"You kidding me? That's the *last* place they'd ever put me." Pat actually smiled for a second. "So what about you?"

"I don't know," Kai said. "Guess I'll stay around here for a while and see what happens."

Pat nodded. "You seem pretty good at taking care of yourself."

Not like I have a choice, Kai thought.

"You're gonna be sixteen," Pat said.

"Yeah."

His father rubbed his hand across his mouth. Kai could hear the older man's palm scrape across the stubble on his jaw. The Alien

Frog Beast seemed to be lost in thought. Then he leaned closer to the Plexiglas. "You know the place where Sean and I moved?"

"Yeah?"

"Go down the wooden stairs in the back. There's a black metal mailbox on the wall next to the door. Inside's the door key. In the bathroom medicine cabinet are some bottles of pills and crap. One of them says vitamin B. Inside's a key to a safe-deposit box for the First Bank of Sun Haven. Box number two-fifty-six."

Kai waited for his father to say something more, but the Alien Frog Beast said nothing.

"That's it?" Kai asked.

"That's it."

"Okay, thanks."

"Stay in touch." His father started to get up.

"I will," said Kai. Pat turned and walked toward the door where a guard stood.

The guard frowned and looked at his watch. "You've still got two minutes."

"That's okay," Kai's father said. "I've got stuff to do."

Thirty-three

It was 6 A.M. and there was just the slightest chill in the air. The grass in front of the L. Balter & Son funeral home was covered by a thick coat of dew and felt cold under Kai's feet. Carried on the offshore breeze, a monarch butterfly glided overhead on fragile wings. Kai had read somewhere that like birds, these butterflies flew south in the fall.

He wondered if he should have put on his wet suit, then decided against it. The water was still warm and despite the morning chill, as soon as the sun came up the day would get hot.

With his board under his arm, Kai walked down to the beach. Bean had decided to sleep in this morning. The waves were small, no more than waist high, but the conditions were perfect—glassy, the offshore breeze steady, the waves peeling off the jetty with almost machinelike precision. When Kai got to the beach, someone else was already in the water. Even from the boardwalk, Kai knew it was Lucas.

By the time Kai kneeled down to wax his board, Lucas was outside, waiting for a wave. Kai stroked the wax on. Thanks to the morning chill it took a little more effort than usual. Out of the corner of his eye, he saw Lucas turn his board toward shore and paddle into a wave. Kai stopped waxing and watched. Lucas popped up, dropped down the small face, then appeared to hesitate for an instant, as if he couldn't decide what to do. Unlike the hard slashing turn Kai was used to seeing, Lucas chose a more relaxed, sweeping course back up the face and over the lip, disappearing behind the wave.

Kai splashed into the water. He paddled out and sat up on his board outside, half a dozen yards from Lucas. They nodded at each other. Kai expected Lucas to remain tight lipped, so he was surprised when he said, "Sorry I couldn't make the party. Something came up."

"Something to do with your father?"

Lucas nodded, then looked around. "Nice day, huh?"

"Be nicer if it was just a little bigger," Kai said.

"Yeah. But hey, when isn't that true?"

"You're right."

A new set was coming. Kai and Lucas let the first wave roll under them. The second wave jacked up nicely. Kai and Lucas exchanged a look. Either of them could have taken it. There was that moment when, if Lucas had wanted the wave, he would have started to turn the nose of his board around. Instead he nodded at Kai. He was giving up the wave. Kai grabbed it.

He took a short ride, kicked out, and paddled back. Once again he and Lucas sat outside, scanning the horizon for the next set. A seagull hovered thirty feet in the air over the jetty and dropped a clam onto the rocks. Then dived down to devour the insides before other seagulls got to it.

"So how're things?" Kai asked.

"Different," said Lucas. "I told my father I want to surf alone from now on."

It was a simple thing to say, but Kai knew it meant a lot.

"Kind of weird about fathers, isn't it?" Lucas asked. "I mean, they work so hard to make you think they're these big heroes. And then one day you wake up and realize it's not true."

"My father was never a hero to me," Kai said. "I just thought I was stuck with him. Your dad may have done some bad stuff, but at least he cares about you."

"Yeah, but there's this deal he expects," said Lucas. "It's like, 'I'll care about you as long as you do what I want you to do.' Then the day comes, you wake up and decide that part's not so important anymore. What's more important is what you want to do, not worrying about what he wants."

"Yeah, I know what you mean," Kai said.

Two guys came down the beach carrying boards. They'd come from the direction of the Driftwood Motel, and stopped on the sand in front of Screamers and started to wax. It was obvious they were gonna paddle out.

"You ever see those two before?" Lucas asked.

Kai nodded. One was the thin guy with tousled blond hair and tattoos on both arms. The other was the stocky guy with dark hair shaved close to his head and black tattoos on both shoulders.

Lucas and Kai watched as the two paddled out, then sat up on their boards nearby. The blond one gave Lucas and Kai a nod. Kai could tell both guys were a little edgy about being out at Screamers.

A good-size set started to come in. It was going to peak closer to where the other two were, but they both glanced at Kai and Lucas to see if either of them would try to claim the wave anyway. Neither Kai nor Lucas budged. It was one of those sets that seemed to look bigger and better the closer it got. Finally the stocky guy with the short black hair shrugged as if to say, *"If you guys don't want to take it, I will."* He turned and paddled into the wave, which by now had jacked up into a beauty. The guy took off, zigging and zagging while Kai and Lucas watched enviously.

"What do you want to bet that was the fricken wave of the day?" Lucas asked.

Kai looked out, hoping to see another one coming, but the rest of the waves in the set were nowhere close to that one.

"Could have been our wave," Lucas said.

"Yeah."

"Now that everyone thinks Screamers is wide open, I bet you'll have to watch a lot of those go by."

"Yeah."

"Tell me it doesn't bother you."

"It bothers me," Kai said. "Believe me, it bothers me."

"But not enough to do anything about it?" Lucas guessed.

"I already did something about it," Kai said.

The frown on Lucas's face turned into a smirk. "Yeah, I guess you did."

Thirty-four

At the First Bank of Sun Haven Kai stood by the open vault door while a woman used the key he'd found in his father's medicine cabinet to open one of many safe-deposit boxes that lined the wall. She pulled out a long, thin rectangular container and handed it to Kai, then led him to a room about the size of a closet, with a desk and a lamp inside.

"I'll wait out here," she said, closing the door.

Kai sat at the desk and turned on the light. He stared down at the gray metal container. He'd already decided that if it contained money, he wasn't going to take it. He lifted the metal lid. Inside was a wrinkled manila envelope held closed by a rubber band.

Kai slid off the rubber band and opened the envelope. Out fell a birth certificate, a folded yellow card with his immunization records, a photo of his mother holding a baby with blue eyes, and a one-way plane ticket to Hawaii.

Kai stared at it all in disbelief. It was almost impossible to accept that the Alien Frog Beast had done this for him. Kai put the papers back into the manila envelope, then placed the envelope in his pocket. He closed the metal container and sat for a long time without moving.

"Is everything okay?" the woman waiting outside asked.

"Yeah." Kai got up and went back out, handing the container to her. A moment later he left the bank and stood on the sidewalk, feeling the sun's rays on his face.

He had a decision to make. A big one. But either way, he had a feeling it was going to be okay.

Todd Strasser is the author of more than one hundred novels for teens and middle graders including the best-selling Help! I'm Trapped In . . . series. His novels for older teens include *The Accident, The Wave, Give a Boy a Gun,* and *Can't Get There from Here.* Todd and his kids have surfed Hawaii, California, and the eastern seaboard from Florida to New York.